Under the Mistletoe

Under the Mistletoe

A Heart of Texas Romance

Eve Gaddy

TULE
PUBLISHING

Chapter One

SPENCER MCBRIDE LOVED Christmas. He especially loved Christmas in Last Stand, Texas. He loved the whole season. The parties, the food and drink, the Christmas trees, the decorations, Santa and his elves, the Christmas market, Christmas carols, presents, mistletoe. If it had to do with Christmas, Spencer loved it.

It wasn't a secret. Everyone who knew Spencer knew he loved Christmas.

The tree-trimming party was an open house at the Corbyn Mansion, and took place every year on the Saturday after Thanksgiving to start off the season. Everyone in town was invited. Trees for people to decorate, each with a different theme, were placed in every room on the ground floor. The whole place was lit up like a—well, a Christmas tree. Emma, Delilah and Amelia Corbyn really knew how to throw a party. Delicious cookies and beverages, alcoholic and non, were set on tables in each room. Since Delilah Corbyn was the chef who owned Dragonfly restaurant, the food was always great.

The Corbyns had outdone themselves this time. Mistletoe hung everywhere. In the doorways, from chandeliers, even in unexpected places like over a couch or hanging from the mantel. He wondered if one of the women had plans and, if so, who they planned to catch. He said as much to his brother Graham and Graham's wife Bella. They were still newlyweds so he figured they'd already scoped out any excuse to kiss.

"What's with the mistletoe?"

"This is my first Corbyn tree-decorating party," Bella said. "Don't they usually have mistletoe?"

"Yes," Graham said.

At the same time both men said, "But not this much."

"Who is that pretty redhead?" Spencer asked catching sight of a woman he didn't know. She wore a long-sleeved, sparkly dark red dress. It hugged her curves lovingly but the best part, in Spencer's opinion, was that it was blessedly short, showing off dynamite legs. You'd think with her red hair, it wouldn't look good, but *Mama Mia*, you'd be wrong.

"I don't know," Graham said. "Do you, Bella?"

Bella shook her head. "I haven't seen her before."

"Neither have I." And he'd have remembered her, that's for damn sure.

He set off to wrangle an intro to the cute redhead. But he couldn't find anyone who knew her. And she'd disappeared. He thought he'd find her in one of the rooms at the Corbyn Mansion, but no luck so far. Maybe she'd left already.

As he left the room someone called his name and said hello. He waved, and looking back over his shoulder, he ran smack into a woman in the doorway. He tried to grab her to steady her, but missed.

"Oh, crap," the redhead said, wiping at her dress ineffectually. He realized her glass of wine was now empty.

Damn. "Totally my fault," he said. "I hope that wasn't red wine."

Looking down, she said, "No, it's white. Or it was. Thank goodness."

Her voice was low-pitched, sweet and warm, a mix of bourbon and honey. Spencer snatched several napkins from a passing waiter. "I'm really sorry. I'll pay for the dry cleaner."

She looked at him then and smiled. "No, it's my fault as much as yours. I wasn't looking where I was going either."

Her eyes were blue. Not plain old blue but a clear blue the color of the Mediterranean at sunrise. Eyes fringed with thick, dark lashes and set in a face with high cheekbones and a mouth made for kissing. He looked upward and smiled.

"What?" She looked up too.

"Mistletoe," Spencer said, pointing upward.

She appeared startled, then flustered. "Uh, I don't think so."

Unsurprised, Spencer laughed. "How about we settle for a handshake?" He held out his hand.

She put her much smaller hand in his and shook with a firm grip. "I'm Georgie Durant."

"Spencer McBride. You must be new in town. Or just visiting." Obviously he hoped she was the former.

"Yes, I'm new. I just moved here about a week ago. Some of my coworkers brought me to the party. I worried I was crashing but—" She shrugged. "They swore it didn't matter."

"Way too many people here to worry about one more. Besides, the Corbyns welcome everyone to the party. It's tradition." Since they still stood in the doorway, he looked up again. "Like mistletoe."

She laughed. "Nice try, but it's still not happening."

He grinned but didn't reply.

Lana Jones, a paramedic he worked with sometimes, stopped to talk to Georgie. After greeting Spencer, she pulled Georgie away with her. Looking over her shoulder, Georgie said, "Nice to meet you. Maybe I'll see you around."

"I can guarantee you will," Spencer muttered to himself.

The next time he saw her she was standing in the doorway of the library. Under the mistletoe. Again. The library was Emma Corbyn's domain, which was reasonable since she was Last Stand's head librarian. Books lined shelves from floor to ceiling. He'd bet his last dollar they were organized just like the public library. There was a huge tree on one side of the room, already partially decorated with lights and some ornaments. A roaring fire, dark wood furniture with red upholstery, and an oriental-style rug gave the room an elegant vibe. Knowing the Corbyn ancestors had been in Last Stand since the Texas Revolution, he knew there were antiques all over the place. Finally, a table with a bunch of kids making something with glue and sparkles completed the picture.

The woman in the doorway made the setting perfection. At least this time he hadn't actually run into her. He walked up behind her and said near her ear, "You're standing under the mistletoe again. Some men might wonder if that was deliberate."

"I am not." Georgie looked up and frowned. "Purely accidental. Besides, it's hard to avoid. And it's still not happening."

"Darn. Oh, well, no harm in trying. I'm Spencer and I'm very single."

Georgie laughed. "Well, that's original. I'll give you that. Most men don't come right out and say it."

"I wanted to be clear, so that you'd know when I ask you out it's legit."

"Hmm."

That was noncommittal. "What about you? Any husband or boyfriend?"

"Oh, I'm single too."

"Great. We have something in common. Besides meeting under the mistletoe."

Just then the carolers came through. Dressed in Victorian period clothes, they circulated through all the rooms singing Christmas carols. Problem was, he turned around and she was gone. Damn, why did she keep disappearing?

Ordinarily he'd have shrugged and taken it as a sign. But there was something about Georgie Durant that intrigued him, so he kept looking.

He poked his head into each room, determined to at least get her phone number the next time he saw her. Unless she'd left already. Luckily, she hadn't. He found her in the foyer, standing under another sprig of mistletoe that hung up high from a chandelier.

"Hi."

"Hi. Why do we keep running into each other?"

"Probably because I've been looking for you. You realize you've done it again, right?"

"Done it again?"

He cast his eyes upward. "You should be more careful. All men aren't as understanding as I am," he added modestly.

She looked up too, and frowned. "Oh, for—I can't go around looking up every time I stop to talk or to glance around a room."

"I suppose not. But you do seem to have a knack for the mistletoe."

"Entirely accidental. I've never been to a party with mistletoe coming out the yin-yang."

Spencer laughed. "Great description. How about we shake hands again? Unless you've changed your mind?" he added, knowing she hadn't.

"You're very persistent, aren't you?"

"You say that like it's a problem." Solemnly, he held out his hand. They shook and he thought again that she had a surprisingly strong grip. Maybe she was a physical therapist.

"So tell me, Georgie Durant, what brought you to Last Stand?"

"A new job. I've been in Houston for the last few years and I needed a change."

"Who do you work for?"

"The fire department. I'm a paramedic."

That explained her grip. Spencer stared at her. He'd been

off for the last week or he'd surely have met her.

"Spencer? Why are you staring at me?"

"Sorry. I was just surprised. I work for the Last Stand Fire Department too. Firefighter paramedic."

"Really? Why haven't I met you? I've been here a week."

"I've been on a break for the last week and out of town. I knew they were looking for another paramedic but no one told me you were the new hire." Which he'd take up with his so-called buddies. "I can see why, of course."

"I don't understand. What does that mean?"

"Are you kidding? A beautiful single woman joins the paramedics and not one of my friends tells me?"

She blushed and laughed. "Beautiful is stretching it but thanks."

He looked at her, taking in the wavy red curls, picture-perfect face and killer body in that sparkly red dress. She was cute, but a beautiful kind of cute. "Nope. If anything, beautiful is an understatement."

🌿

"WANT TO GO sit somewhere and talk for a while?" Spencer asked.

Spencer might not have heard of her, but she'd heard of him. Earlier, when she asked Marcella Henderson, the friend who'd brought her to the party, about him Marcella's response had been, "Spencer McBride? Yeah, he's a great guy. Great-looking. Hot. A bit of a flirt but he's a lot of fun. Why?"

"No reason. I ran into him earlier tonight. Literally ran into him."

Marcella laughed. "That's a novel way to meet a guy."

"Tell me about it." A flirt who's a lot of fun. Well, that had warned her off. But still, she admitted to curiosity. Surely it wouldn't hurt to simply talk to him. She was going to work with him, after all.

He led her to a sofa in one of the less busy rooms. She wasn't sure what they called this room. There were so many rooms she couldn't keep up. Only a few other people were in there and they were over by the tree, talking. The room was small and cozy, with dark wood furniture and a blazing fireplace, a parquet floor with a beautiful Aubusson carpet and a smaller tree that was mostly decorated by now. And cookies and beverages set out on a table.

"Do you want a cookie?" Spencer asked her.

"Yes, how did you know?"

He was grinning widely. "You had a gleam in your eyes that said, 'Chocolate. I must have chocolate.'"

"What are you, a mind reader?"

"No, but I know a fellow chocolate lover when I see one." He got up, walked to the table and came back with cookies—chocolate, naturally—on a paper plate. He took one and handed her the plate.

She took one, bit into it and nearly moaned with pleasure. "Oh, my God, this is so good."

"Courtesy of Delilah Corbyn. She owns Dragonfly restaurant."

"I'll have to try it out if these cookies are an indication of her food."

"Trust me, the rest of their food is great too." He leaned back and relaxed. Casually dressed in a pair of dark slacks and a button-down, long-sleeved dark green shirt, he was something to look at.

Stop drooling, idiot. So he's cute. Big deal.

"So, Georgie, tell me about you. You said you left your last job because you needed something different. Why did you choose Last Stand?"

She had to finish the cookie before she could speak. Which gave her time to consider her answer. She sure as hell wasn't going to tell him she'd left primarily because of a failed love affair. No, that was a tidbit she'd keep to herself, thank you very much. "Partly because they had an opening. Partly because a friend of mine who used to live here told me I'd love it here. But mostly because I wanted out of Houston and the Hill Country has always seemed like a great place to live. I've visited the area a few times over the years. When I seriously considered moving, I stayed in Fredericksburg for a while and visited Last Stand. I really liked it here, so I took the job when they offered."

"All very good reasons. We're lucky to have you."

"How do you know that? You haven't worked with me yet."

"Because the department wouldn't have hired you otherwise."

"Oh." She hadn't thought of it that way. "Are you a local?"

"Born and raised," he said with a nod. "I left for a while

for training and worked for a year and a half in Dallas but I came back. My entire family is here."

"I met a Dr. McBride. I'm guessing he's your brother? He was with the woman who owns the pie shop. Charlie, I think she said."

"That's Turner. I have two brothers, both doctors. My dad is a retired GP."

"I've heard about him too. Everyone speaks so highly of him."

"Yup. I'm the renegade. Well, besides my sister Jessie. She raises mustangs."

"Oh, you have a ranch?"

"My family does. Jessie runs it now, with some help from our mother."

"So your sister's a cowgirl. Are you a cowboy?"

He laughed. "Not anymore. I still ride. And help Jessie with the horses, mostly when I can't get out of it."

"You said you were a renegade. Is that because you're not a doctor?"

"Right. I like medicine but all those years of school were not my thing."

"You need education to be a firefighter paramedic."

"True. But not twelve years of it. I wanted to get on with my career but I still wanted to be involved with medicine."

"Good point. So you're happy with your career?"

"I love it," he said simply.

That was refreshing to hear. A lot of people at her last job weren't happy. But they wouldn't do anything to change it. They just complained. "How do you split up your work?

I'm so new I don't really know much about how the department works. I've only been out on a few calls, and they were with Marcella."

"Marcella's good. But the whole department is good. You'll like working here." He reached over and took another cookie. When he finished he said, "You asked how it works. We—those of us who are also firefighters—rotate through. We have set days, but we also can work with whoever needs us. Whether it's fire department or EMS."

"So you and I will be working together some?"

"We will." He studied her for a moment. "Why, is that a problem for you?"

"No. Of course not," she said hastily. Except for the fact that she had decided when she left Houston that she was never going to date a coworker again. And she had a feeling he was going to ask her out. After all, he'd said as much. If he did?

Then you say thanks but no thanks.

But he's so cute. And funny. And...

"I think I heard a *but* in there."

He was entirely too appealing. And she was a sucker for a pretty face. Which brought to mind thoughts of Cole Baxter, her ex-boyfriend, which she resolutely banished. Much better to think of Spencer, even if she was going to work with him. And speaking of pretty faces.

It really is a gorgeous face. He could be an actor. Or a model. And he seems so nice.

I'm sure he is. Nice and flirtatious.

Oh, give the guy a break. He's young and single. Nothing

wrong with flirting.

Still, I know that type.

You're judging him before you even know him.

Yeah. So?

"Why do I get the feeling I've been assessed and came up lacking?"

She blushed. Damn, she'd blushed more with this man in an evening than she had for the entire last year. "Nothing of the sort. We just met."

"You look worried."

He really was a mind reader.

"I have an idea," Spencer said when she didn't answer. "What are your feelings about gingerbread houses?"

"To eat or to decorate?"

"Decorate, although I'm sure there will be edible decorations left over. In the dining room there are gingerbread houses made like the Corbyn Mansion. We can see if there are any left to decorate."

"That sounds like fun."

As she'd expected, the dining room was a huge, formal affair with a dining table big enough to seat at least twelve. Gingerbread houses in the shape of the mansion were placed all over the room, with a few that hadn't been decorated yet set out on the table. Against the large windows was a tall Christmas tree, which as far as she could tell, was completely decorated with lights, glass and wooden ornaments, and candy canes.

They decided to each take a side of the house and decorate it. "Don't you think it will look weird if we each do our own thing?" she asked.

"Maybe. Let's find out."

There was icing in every color you could imagine. There were gumdrops, candy canes, peppermint candies, sparkles and glitter. Georgie and Spencer stood side by side, occasionally reaching for the same decoration and laughing each time it happened. Georgie went heavy on the icing and the glitter, with some candy hearts and red hots candy accenting windows and doors. Spencer went for the gumdrops, peppermints, and candy canes, and used the icing as an accent.

When they finished they stood back to see their whole creation.

Georgie burst out laughing. "Oh, my God," she said when she could manage. "It looks *terrible*!"

"It's not terrible. It's unique," Spencer said. He frowned at her and added, "Don't diss our offspring."

That set her off again. After she gained control, she said, "That thing is no offspring of mine."

"Hush, you'll hurt its feelings."

"Gingerbread houses don't have feelings."

"Of course they do. It's Christmas. Christmas magic." He looked at the house again. "I do think you went a little overboard with the icing."

"Me? You used so many gumdrops and candy canes, I'm surprised it isn't listing to that side."

"You have icing on your cheek," he said. "And on your nose. And I swear I think there's some in your hair."

She gaped at him. "I do not!" Or did she?

"Don't take my word for it. Besides, it's cute."

"I'm going to the ladies' room," she said loftily.

"Are you coming back?"

"You'll have to wait and see."

It took her a few minutes to find the restroom, which was tucked away behind the double stairway in the foyer. Damn it, he was right. She had icing from stem to stern. Cute? He thought it was cute? She thought she looked like a goof.

When she emerged from the restroom, she didn't have far to go to find Spencer. He was standing a few feet away, underneath the grand staircase, talking to a very pretty brunette in a short green dress. She left him as Georgie came up to them.

"I didn't mean to chase away your friend."

"You didn't. That was my sister, making me promise to ride one of her horses tomorrow. I don't start work until Monday."

Work. Oh, yeah. She was going to be working with him. But she wasn't yet. "You were right. I had icing everywhere."

"Not everywhere. But I don't lie. Usually."

"Good to know. You said usually. When do you lie?"

"Only white lies so I don't hurt someone's feelings. Like when a woman asks, 'Does this dress make me look fat?' To which the answer is always and forever 'no.' Only a fool would answer that truthfully, especially if it did."

"And you're no fool, I take it."

"I try hard not to be. But look, the mistletoe gods have spoken."

She laughed. "There are no mistletoe gods."

"Yes there are. The night is almost over. This is the fifth time we've met under the mistletoe."

She looked up. Damn, he was right. This was getting ridiculous. "Did you plan this one?" she asked suspiciously.

"Yes. I wanted to kiss you."

Well, he'd owned up to that one. Maybe he was right. If they kissed and got it over with then she could put him firmly in the friend camp. Besides, it wasn't a big deal. One kiss, in public. What could go wrong? She looked at him and said, "Okay."

"Such enthusiasm."

"Take it or leave it."

"Oh, I'll definitely go for it." He cupped her face in his hands, looking down at her with a smile.

Damn, his eyes were green. A beautiful dark green. Like an emerald only deeper. Mesmerizing.

He kissed her. He didn't touch her anywhere but her face and her lips. It started out chaste and sweet. Then she opened her mouth and touched her tongue to his. Which was a stupid thing to do but she did it. He didn't take advantage. Just continued to kiss her, his tongue only flirting with hers. But oh, what would it be like to really kiss him?

He drew back, his hands still on her face. He looked the way she felt. Bowled over.

Chapter Two

THE NEXT DAY Spencer went out to the ranch to ride one of Jessie's horses. Since the mare—a rescue—was still a bit skittish around men, she wanted one of her brothers to ride her. Spencer didn't mind. He could ride almost any horse Jessie could ride—not that he'd ever admit there was a horse she could ride and he couldn't. He liked to ride and didn't manage it often enough to suit him.

When he was younger he'd even considered raising horses. That was Jessie's dream, and Spencer loved horses too. Not as much as his sister did, true, but he could see himself getting into it. But the lure of medicine was too strong and once he figured out he could achieve his goal a lot faster by becoming a paramedic rather than a doctor, he was hooked.

He wondered whether Jessie wanted to ride in the field or the round pen. He hoped it was the field. It was a gorgeous, clear and chilly day. Luckily Jessie wanted to check fence lines. As they saddled the horses he asked, "What's the mare's name?"

"Nellie."

"Nellie? You're kidding."

Jessie shrugged. "She had another name but she didn't

like it. So I named her Nellie. She looks like a Nellie."

He supposed she did. They finished saddling up and rode out to check the fence lines.

"How was the party?" Jessie asked.

"It was good. As always. But you were there. Why are you asking me?"

"Because I wanted the scoop on the cute redhead I saw you kissing shortly after I left you. I've never seen her before. Who is she?"

"Her name's Georgie Durant. She's a new paramedic. Just moved here about a week ago."

"You work fast. You just blew back into town a day or two ago."

He shot his sister a glance. She hadn't said it with any particular inflection. Yet he felt compelled to defend himself. "Not really. That was the fifth time we met under the mistletoe. How could I miss those signs?"

And oh, my God, what a kiss it had been. He was still wondering what the hell had happened to him. It was a kiss. A simple kiss. It shouldn't have meant anything. It hadn't meant anything.

So why was he still thinking about it and still blown away by it?

"Spencer? It must have been some kiss."

He shrugged. "Just a kiss under the mistletoe."

"Right," Jessie said, drawing out the word.

Spencer liked women. All women. Which meant he saw no reason to tie himself down to only one. He was only twenty-eight. Plenty of time to settle down later.

He dated and was faithful to the woman he was with, but somehow those things never lasted for long. The last woman he'd dated for any length of time was Regina. She'd broken up with him when she decided to go back to her old boyfriend.

He hadn't minded. Truthfully, he'd been ready to let her go too.

He just hadn't gotten around to it.

"There's a break. Dang, there's always a break," Jessie said.

"Want me to go back and get the truck?" The truck had all the equipment to mend the fence. Extra wire, the come-along, heavy gloves—whatever you needed to mend fences and a lot more.

"No, I've got a new hand who says he can do it. Since this is one of my least favorite chores, I want to see if he really can."

The mare shied. "Whoa there, Nellie." He reined her in and patted her neck, looking around to see what had spooked the horse. "I can't tell you how stupid I feel saying that."

"I like it," Jessie said. "I think it was that plastic bag that scared her." She motioned to the bag now caught on the fence.

"Better that than a snake."

"A snake? At this time of year? I doubt it."

"Hey, it's a sunny day and you know rattlers don't really hibernate."

"You never have gotten over being bitten by a rattlesnake, have you?"

He'd been about twelve when he'd surprised a rattler. "I've gotten over it. I just don't want to do it again."

"Can't blame you. It didn't look like fun."

"It wasn't."

"Are you going to ask her out?"

"Who?" he asked, accustomed to his sister's rapid change of subjects.

"Your mistletoe kiss, who else?"

"Maybe."

He wanted to get to know Georgie Durant better. Hell, he wanted to see if that kiss had been a fluke. He couldn't blame it on alcohol since he only had one beer the entire night. He suspected the kiss had affected her too. She'd looked shell-shocked afterward.

Just like he had, he imagined.

"I thought you'd sworn off dating coworkers?"

"I'm not dating her. Yet."

"I knew that wouldn't last long."

"Generally, it's a mistake to date a coworker but I can make an exception."

"Yes, but will she?"

"Won't know until I ask." Crap. It would be just his luck if Georgie had a rule against dating coworkers. Well, if she did, he'd just have to change her mind.

❧

MONDAY MORNING GEORGIE went to work, excited because

she was on a regular rotation now instead of the one she thought of as "getting to know you." She'd met all of the paramedics and most of the firefighters the week before.

"What's this?" Georgie asked Marcella, who was standing in front of the bulletin board. There was a note pinned to the board that read, "Toy drive meeting today at four p.m."

"What?"

Georgie pointed to the note. "That. Toy drive?"

"Oh, that. The fire department hosts a toy drive every year. This meeting is to assign the people in charge and the other volunteers. It's a big deal around here. We take care of a lot of kids from the rural communities all around us. Including Last Stand, of course."

"What if you're out on a call during the meeting?"

Marcella grinned. "Then you'll get stuck with a job for sure. There's always one person from the fire department and one from the paramedics who are in charge of the whole thing."

"Why are you grinning?"

"Because Spencer McBride is always the firefighter in charge of it."

"So?"

"So I'm betting you'll be the person from the paramedics."

"Why me?"

"You're the newest here for one thing. It will make you become a part of the community quicker. Plus," she added with a wink, "I saw you kissing him under the mistletoe at the Corbyns' party."

"That was nothing," she said quickly. Which was a big fat lie. That kiss had been amazing. Or it seemed that way at the time. Still, it was one kiss and they were coworkers now. So she might as well forget it. She'd over-romanticized the whole thing for sure.

Keep telling yourself that.

I'm sure he didn't feel like I did about that kiss. Did he?

"It looked like something to me," Marcella said. "But whatever you say."

Sure enough, Georgie was working at four p.m. and by the time she returned it was after five-thirty. She'd mostly forgotten about the toy drive when she heard a couple of people standing by the bulletin board say something about it. She walked over to look and wasn't really surprised to find she'd been named the paramedic in charge. Was it Spencer's doing?

She went looking for him and found him just getting back from a fire. Oh, God, he looked hot. Hot as in damn good, although he looked hot temperature wise from working a fire too. He still wore his Nomex pants but the suspenders hung down from his waist and he'd taken off the jacket and wore only a short-sleeved navy T-shirt that stretched tight over a broad chest and muscular arms. Telling herself that most firefighters were built like that, or developed those kinds of muscles from their work, didn't help a bit. Even reminding herself that her ex-boyfriend had similar muscles didn't help. She still wanted to drool.

"Bad fire?" she asked him.

"Not for people, thank God. It was a brush fire on the

edge of town."

"Then who was it bad for?"

"Wildlife," he said shortly. "What can I do for you, Georgie?"

Well, damn, he has a soft spot for animals too. This guy is too good to be for real. Maybe. According to gossip he's a flirt and dates a lot of women.

What young, single firefighter you know doesn't?

Good point. And really, do I care?

No, but she'd just left a job where she'd been involved with a coworker and then things went south. And she didn't want to do that again.

She asked, more brusquely than she intended, "Did you pick me to be the paramedic in charge of the toy drive? Your counterpart in our department?"

He looked confused and then grinned. "I wasn't even at the meeting. Relax, it's probably because you're a newbie here."

"Is it that hard of a job?"

Spencer shrugged, which made his muscles ripple.

Jeez, there oughtta be a law.

"Obviously, I don't think so. I do it every year. Look, if it's that big of a deal go cross out your name and we'll find someone else."

"And look like Scrooge? No thanks. I just wondered if you had—" She stopped abruptly, aware she was about to accuse him of engineering something he'd clearly had no part in.

"If I'd arranged it so we could work together? No, but I

might have if I'd have thought about it."

"Why?"

"Why not?"

She had no answer to that.

"Are you worried about this because we kissed under the mistletoe? You're afraid I'm going to hit on you?"

Damn her fair skin. She knew she blushed. "Of course not."

"Good. Because I won't kiss you again." He paused and added with a wicked smile, "Unless you want me to."

Georgie gaped at him. "Better corral that ego, cowboy."

"Yes, ma'am," he drawled, and saluted her.

She gave him the evil eye but it didn't appear to bother him.

"Meeting tonight at seven. Here. I'm cooking so all you need to do is show up."

"I'll bring brownies. How many people?"

"Ten or twelve besides us. Depends on who signed up."

"I never signed up."

"Somebody did it for you. And no, it wasn't me. See you later," he said and strode off, likely to take a shower.

Which brought to mind another scenario she had no business thinking about. She had to get hold of herself. If they were going to work together she needed to start thinking of him as a friend. Not a sexy, fascinating man.

And that was going to be damn near impossible.

Chapter Three

S PENCER LOVED THE toy drive. His sister Jessie told him that was because he was like a kid about Christmas himself. So sue him. He enjoyed the season. He got a kick out of seeing the toys people donated and he really liked seeing the kids' faces when they realized the toys were for them. Some of them had never had a new toy. Hell, some of the kids had never had a real toy at all. It made him happy to be able to bring some joy into the kids' lives.

He had a system, perfected—well, almost—over the last few years since he'd first volunteered to run the drive. The Daughters of Last Stand service organization always took care of collecting the kids' names and what they wanted or needed. There was a printer in town who donated his time and equipment to make flyers and posters. At Spencer's insistence, LSFD paid for the paper and poster boards but Mr. Penny covered the labor and production costs. *The Defender*, Last Stand's newspaper, ran a free ad for the drive every day in the lead-up, listing drop-off locations, the dates of the toy drive, and most desired gifts.

The group that met to hash out the details was loud and raucous, consisting of fire and EMS people, and most of them knew each other well. There were several people who worked both fire and EMS as well as people who only worked one or the other. Spencer made spaghetti and meat sauce, since he could easily make enough to feed a whole bunch of people. He threw in some crusty French bread and a green salad and called it a meal.

Georgie brought brownies as she'd promised. They were gone as soon as Georgie put them out. He managed to snare one before she set them out and was sorry he hadn't taken more.

Spencer knew that no matter what they said or what their intentions were, not everyone would follow through with their part in the toy drive. Shit happened. He was used to it. But as long as his counterpart among the paramedics contributed, and with the help of at least a few other people, the toy drive was always a success. Some years were better than others, of course.

He noticed his buddy, Cable Jackson, had managed to sit next to Georgie and was regaling her with, he suspected, mostly fictional stories of his adventures. Georgie was laughing and he thought again how pretty she was.

After they split up the workload and people were milling around, Spencer noticed Cable looking at Georgie with a mystified expression. He walked over to him and said, "Struck out, I take it."

Cable shrugged. "Yeah. One minute we're having a great time and then after I asked her out she blew me off."

"What did she say?"

"That she doesn't date coworkers. I told her we weren't

really coworkers since I'm a firefighter and she's a paramedic but she still said no."

"I thought you were still with Marcella? What's up with that?"

"She broke it off." He shrugged as if it didn't matter but Spencer knew it did. Cable had been hung up on Marcella for a long time.

"Did you screw up?" Cable had a tendency to shoot himself in the foot when it came to women. He probably had, he thought when his buddy denied it and changed the subject.

"No, Marcella screwed up. But we were talking about the new hire. Rumor has it you two were gettin' it on at the Corbyns' tree-trimming party. You're a coworker. How did you rate?"

"We weren't getting it on. It was just a kiss." An amazing kiss but his buddy didn't need to know that. "And I haven't asked her out."

"Did you set it up for her to be the paramedic in charge of the toy drive?"

"No. That was just luck."

"You always have been a lucky bastard."

Several people signed up to check and unload some of the barrels, but the remainder went to Spencer and Georgie. Plus they had to cover for anyone who couldn't manage because of work.

"Great brownies," he told Georgie.

"Thanks. They're pretty much my only domestic talent."

"Really? You only have one?"

"Pretty much," she repeated. "Alas, I'm no domestic

goddess."

"You're a paramedic. You don't need to be a domestic goddess as well."

"True but sometimes I wish I was a little more talented in that direction. I do make a mean peanut butter and jelly sandwich, though."

He laughed. "You've got my sister Jessie beat. If it isn't a horse or something related to horses she doesn't give a rip about it. She could truly burn water if any of us were crazy enough to ask her to cook."

"Since she's a horsewoman I'd say she doesn't need to be a cook either."

"You got that right." His sister could do anything she set her mind to. Cooking wasn't on her list of necessary evils. She either ate what someone else cooked or scrounged for food. "I should introduce you two. You'd like each other."

"I'd like that. I'm always up for meeting new people."

He filed that away to talk to Jessie about. Spencer generally spent the afternoon and evening prior to the start of the drive getting set up to collect the toys. "Looks like tomorrow we need to distribute the flyers and the barrels."

"I can do that. Do you always put the barrels in the same place?"

"Some of them. Some of them rotate. We reassess yearly to see which ones get the most action and change location accordingly."

Georgie fished her phone out of her pocket and looked at the readout. "I need to take this." She walked out of the galley, returning a short time later.

"Sorry, I didn't mean to cut you off. That was my sister's daily call."

"I hope everything is okay."

"Oh, it's fine. Erin's first baby is due in a few weeks and she's convinced she's going to come early. So Erin calls me every day with an update." She laughed and added, "Sometimes several times a day."

"Congratulations. Is this the first time you'll be an aunt?"

"Yes. I only have the one sister. Erin is a couple of years older than me. She lives in Fort Worth."

"Is she having a difficult pregnancy?"

"No, but she miscarried the first time she got pregnant and she's nervous so we talk a lot. We're close, even though we haven't lived in the same town for years." She sighed and added, "I was born and raised in Fort Worth and my family is still there. They wanted me to come back to Fort Worth when I left Houston, but this was a better job than I could find back home. And besides, as I told you before, I wanted something different. And I discovered I liked the Hill Country."

"Good. The Hill Country likes you too."

She laughed. "We'll see about that. But I hope you're right."

SPENCER DIDN'T SEE Georgie until late afternoon the day after the organizational meeting at the fire station. It was all he could do not to do a double take when he saw her. Tight jeans, scuffed red cowboy boots, obviously broken in, a red turtleneck sweater that molded to her figure and her leather jacket slung over her arm was a picture that while nice, shouldn't have knocked him for a loop. But it had. Maybe it was simply Georgie who knocked him for a loop. Ever since that kiss...

Nope. Forget that. You said you wouldn't kiss her again until she wanted you to do it. Which could be never.

"Hi," she said. "Where do we start?"

"Main Street," he replied, handing her a bundle of flyers. "You handle those and I'll put up the posters in the windows. Almost everyone lets me do that and the few who won't will at least distribute the flyers."

"How many do I give each business?"

"At least ten. More if they request them. Mr. Penny can make more as needed."

"More? There are a ton of them here. You think we'll need more?"

"Yup. We hand them out like candy. Especially at the Last Stand Country Christmas Market this weekend. And at every other event any of us attend. We usually get a big rush of presents on the last day, which is next Sunday."

"Why is the toy drive over so long before Christmas?"

"We have to have time to sort the toys, wrap them, and get them and the party ready for the kids."

"Oh. I should have thought of that."

"Have you ever taken part in a toy drive before?"

"No, never. This is a new experience for me."

"You'll enjoy it. At least, I hope you will. We hold the

gift-giving party on Christmas Eve day at the station house. We move the trucks out and hold it in the bay. It's the only place big enough. We've set up a room to store the toys and get everything ready. We're supposed to wrap and tag as the gifts come in, but—" He made a "what are you gonna do" gesture with his hands.

"Hardly anyone wraps the toys and tags them," she said, "so we have to do it all after the drive is over. Right?"

"You got it," he said with a grin. "The first time we didn't wrap them, but just handed them out. But the kids were disappointed to not get a wrapped present. We found that out from one of the little ones."

"They do tend to be more honest."

"Don't I know it. Anyway, now we wrap them. The bakeries donate their specialties for the party, the grocery store handles the soft drinks, and we have a supplier for the Christmas wrap as well."

"Sounds like y'all go all out for Christmas."

"We do. I'll tell you about some of the events but first we need to hit the shops on Main Street, then we'll go out to the grocery store and other places that aren't on the main drag. We try to put advertisements anywhere people will see the flyers and posters."

They started on Main Street. It took them a while to put up the posters and hand out the flyers. Mostly because they hit every shop or eating establishment on Main Street. Spencer noticed that Georgie already knew a lot of the shop owners. She was going to have no trouble at all fitting into Last Stand.

After they'd taken care of Main Street, they distributed the barrels. Then more flyers to a variety of locations. There were some places off Main, a few restaurants here and there, the grocery store and a few other locations farther out of town. The fire station itself had a huge bin which was emptied every morning and the toys were stored for later.

"How often do you check all the barrels?" Georgie asked.

"Daily. The timing varies depending on our work schedules. We take all the toys to the fire station."

"Daily? You must get a lot of toys."

"The citizens of Last Stand are very generous."

"They're certainly nice and welcoming. I know small towns are supposed to be like that but having never lived in one I hadn't experienced it."

"It's a great place. Even though there are basically no secrets. And you haven't met *The Matchmaker* yet."

"I've heard about her, though. Clara Perkins, isn't it?"

"Yes. So she hasn't found you a match yet?"

"No, but I haven't actually met her. Is it true your brother Graham and his wife met through her?"

He grinned. "True as can be. They met at Minna Herdmann's yearly birthday bash."

She looked confused so he explained about the Last Stand matriarch's yearly birthday party. "It's a birthday party for our oldest resident. Minna's an institution around here. One hundred and two and still going strong."

"Wow, how long has the town been doing that?"

"We started when she turned ninety-five. Whoever feared Minna wouldn't live much longer obviously knew nothing about her. Minna's from an earlier generation, and she is as tough as they come."

"You sound fond of her. And proud."

He shrugged. "Everyone around here is."

"I guess you've managed to avoid The Matchmaker?"

"Are you kidding? No, I haven't. Clara's had me going out with almost every single female in town."

"But none of them have stuck."

"Not yet. But you never know." As they drove out to the grocery store he glanced at her. Damn, she was pretty. But he'd found that dating coworkers could get sticky. Regretfully. Still, for her he might be willing to chance a little stickiness. Of course, that assumed he could talk her into dating a coworker, which, according to Cable, she didn't want to do either.

Why was he so gung ho about getting Georgie to go out with him? He didn't usually go to that much trouble for a woman. Was it simply because she was elusive or was there another reason?

"Want to get some Mexican food after we hit the grocery store? I'm starving."

"Look, Spencer, I like you but I don't want you to get the wrong idea. I don't date coworkers."

Exactly what she'd told Cable. "It's not a date." He held up his hand when she started to argue. "If you're going to refuse food every time we are together working on the toy drive you're going to get awfully hungry."

She seemed to think about that. Shrugging she said, "Okay. I could do with Mexican food and a beer."

His kind of woman, he thought but knew better than to say it.

Owned by the Valencia family, Valencia's was the best Mexican food restaurant around. Tex-Mex food at its finest, it had even been written up in magazines as the best place for Mexican food in the entire area. Spencer knew the family well. The Valencias had been there from the beginning, when Last Stand was only a wide spot in the road and a saloon. During the Texas Revolution the Texians from the area had holed up in the saloon and held off a contingent of Santa Anna's army. There were still bullet holes in the Last Stand Saloon's walls from the battle. The Valencias themselves had been firmly with the Texians and fighting against Santa Anna's much larger conquering army.

"I haven't been here yet," Georgie said.

"Then you've been missing the best Tex-Mex in this part of Texas." He opened the door for her and followed her inside. "Georgie Durant, this is Elena de la Cova, the manager of Valencia's. Elena, Georgie's a new paramedic in town and she's never been to your place."

"We're so glad you came in," Elena said after shaking hands with Georgie. "Let me show you to your table."

"What happened to Rosalina?" he asked, referring to the hostess.

"Out sick," Elena said. "I'm taking over hostess duties for the night."

"Esteban here?" he asked her as she led them to a table. Esteban Valencia was the owner and an old friend of Spencer's. They'd gone to high school together.

"Not at the moment but he should be here soon. I'll tell him you're here. I know he'll want to say hello." She left them with menus and told them their server would be with them soon. As soon as she left a teenager brought chips, two bowls of hot sauce and water.

"Do you eat that much hot sauce?"

"Yes, but this one—" he gestured to the bowl closest to him "—is extra spicy. Want some?"

"No, thanks. I don't mind some spice but I don't like it so hot it burns my mouth and opens up my sinuses even when it's lukewarm." Georgie opened the menu and looked it over. "What's good to eat here?"

"Do you like queso?"

"Who doesn't?"

He smiled. "The Valencias are known for their queso. It's an old family recipe that only a Valencia is allowed to make. Lots of people have tried to imitate it but there's some secret ingredient that gives it a unique flair."

"A secret ingredient? That sounds very mysterious. Is it really that good?"

"Wait until you taste it and you can tell me."

"You've certainly piqued my interest. What else is good?"

"Everything. But I usually get the Valencia—the enchilada plate with a little bit of everything."

"How are the fajitas?"

"Great, but everything on the menu is good. I've liked everything I've tried. I don't like mole, so I haven't tried it, but I hear it's good."

Most of the staff was connected in some way to the Valencia family, either a relative or a family friend. Tonight Juana was their waitress. Spencer ordered queso, and then they both ordered their main dish. As usual, Spencer ordered the Valencia plate.

"I'll take the fajitas. Chicken, please," Georgie said. "What beer do you have on tap?"

Juana named an American beer and a Mexican beer. Georgie took the Mexican beer.

Spencer ordered the enchilada plate and the same beer. "Here I thought you were a traditionalist," he said to Georgie after Juana left.

"I am," she said, reaching for a chip and dipping it in hot sauce before eating it. "What makes you think I'm not?"

"You didn't get American beer."

Georgie laughed. "That hardly makes me nontraditional. I'm pretty boring."

"Somehow, Georgie, I don't believe that."

GEORGIE GLANCED AROUND the room. In many ways Valencia's looked like a number of Mexican food places where she'd eaten in the past. The restaurant was in an adobe building, which according to the history written on the back of the menu was a hundred years old. Obviously, it had been kept in good shape all those years. On the walls were large round discs of gold and black, of an Aztec-looking pattern. Colorful sombreros also hung on the wall. One wall was brick with large windows, and in one corner of the main room was an adobe fireplace. There were tables scattered around the center of the room, and carved wood booths with brown leather seats along the edges. The wall at one end of their booth was lined with colorful Mexican tile, with a copper coating below it. "This tile is beautiful," Georgie said, looking at the patterned mix of bright colors. "Do you suppose it came from Mexico?"

"Nope, it's Valencia tile, made in the USA. One branch of the family owns the restaurant, the other manufactures tile. I went to high school with Esteban Valencia, the owner of the restaurant. You'll meet him later. Elena, Esteban's cousin who you just met, comes from the Valencia tile side of the family but she manages the restaurant."

"So it really is a family affair."

"Oh, yeah. Pretty much everyone who works here is some kind of family connection. Even down to the kids who bus the tables and bring chips to the dishwashers, busboys, and servers. Esteban is the eldest of six. Several of the older kids are also involved with the restaurant in some manner. And speaking of Esteban," Spencer said with a grin, "here he comes now."

Spencer stood and exchanged handshakes and back slaps with a man who was frankly gorgeous. Black hair, unexpectedly blue eyes and a blinding smile almost knocked her over when he turned to greet her. Spencer introduced them and Esteban held out a hand. "Welcome to Last Stand, Georgie. How are you liking the town?"

His voice was deep and almost hypnotic. Since they'd been friends in high school, she assumed he and Spencer were about the same age. Belatedly realizing she'd been staring at him without answering his question she responded. "I like it a lot. Your restaurant is lovely."

"Thank you. So are you."

She nearly blushed. "Thank you." Damn, the man oozed charm. She glanced at Spencer, who looked resigned.

The two men spoke for a short while and Esteban left, after telling them the queso was on the house.

"He's very...nice," she said, rather lamely.

Spencer laughed. "I've been watching Esteban's effect on women since high school. No, he's not married, and yes, he's a good guy, and yes, he's most definitely a player."

"I didn't ask."

"You wanted to."

Unable to deny it, she laughed. "I take it that's a common reaction."

"Yeah. I like him anyway."

"Poor baby. You're hardly one to talk." Spencer might not be quite as jaw-droppingly gorgeous as Esteban but she knew he had his fair share of female admirers. She'd already heard them speculating about who he was going to date next and wondering when he was going to settle down like his brothers had. The consensus on that seemed to be *not anytime soon*.

Unabashed, Spencer grinned. "I try but I run a poor second."

Their food came and as promised, the queso was extraordinary and the rest of the food was delicious as well. They sat talking after dinner since unlike many Mexican restaurants

Valencia's was fairly quiet. The more Georgie was around Spencer the more she relaxed. The more she liked him. *Tread carefully*, she told herself. Spencer had a dangerous charm of his own. She'd realized that from the moment they met, under the mistletoe at the Corbyns' party. *Remember that, Georgie. Charming men are your downfall.*

If only she didn't remember that kiss almost every time she looked at him, or feel that frisson of sexual awareness whenever they touched, being careful would have been a lot easier.

Chapter Four

THE CHRISTMAS PARADE took place on the Friday morning of the first full weekend of December. Luckily, Georgie had Friday and Saturday off and didn't have to work again until Sunday. Friday night the lighting of the huge tree in front of the library was slated to take place, with the Christkindlmarkt—the German market honoring the town's German heritage—in full swing that evening. The market—the Last Stand Country Christmas Market—would continue the following two days, with more booths and all kinds of food, toys, handmade gifts, Christmas ornaments and Texas memorabilia for sale. Georgie hadn't been to either of those types of events since she was a kid. She was looking forward to the day and evening and more of the market the next day.

All in all, December was a very busy month for Last Stand.

According to the flyers she'd seen posted around town, the parade started on Wisteria Lane, between the hospital and the Millennial Village apartments. It proceeded down Laurel Street, then hooked a left onto Main Street, which was closed to all but the parade and pedestrian traffic from very early Friday morning to the end of the market on

Sunday evening.

Main Street's decorations had gone up immediately after Thanksgiving. Garlands were wrapped around light poles and Christmas images made with lighted and wrapped wires were stretched across the street on every block. Most of the poles had bows of red, green, or red and white striped ribbons tied at the top.

Georgie tried to watch the parade, but she hadn't gotten there early enough, so she was toward the back of a number of people. While she wasn't extremely short, she was of medium height. Okay, maybe medium to short-ish. Unless she got out front with the kids, she couldn't see. She might as well go home. She was standing on tiptoe and trying to see around people when she heard a man say, "Come with me. You need a better vantage point."

Surprised, she turned around. "Spencer? I'd love to see better. But how?"

He led her to Yippee Ki Yay—the western store selling everything from hats to boots and everything in between. He introduced Georgie to the woman who greeted them. "Georgie, this is Lilly Corbyn. She owns this place. Lilly, meet Georgie Durant. Georgie's a new paramedic in town."

"Welcome to Last Stand, Georgie. Take her up to the roof, Spencer."

"Thanks. She couldn't see a thing outside."

Lilly gave her a sympathetic smile. "I can't ever see at things like that either. I always think if I was just a few inches taller…"

Georgie laughed. "I hear you. I can't tell you how many

times I've thought that."

"Come down for some cider after the parade."

"Sounds great," Spencer said. "Thanks, we'll do that."

He showed her to some stairs and took her out on the flat roof of the store, decorated like it was a balcony rather than a rooftop, with Christmas lights and other decorations. "Oh, this is so cute. Why are we the only ones up here?"

"Someone else will be along soon, I'm sure. Lilly only lets newbies up here during the parade, so they can get a good view of everything. Everyone else has to fend for themselves."

And it was a perfect view. There were floats, decorated as train engines or Christmas trees, or with candy canes and gumdrops. There was one with gingerbread people and a gingerbread house. The floats were all lit with Christmas lights outlining them, as were some of the vintage cars. The mayor rode in a convertible with rather garish lights, Georgie thought. The Peach Queen also had a float, which looked like a peach tree complete with ornaments as well as peaches. The queen, wearing a peach dress with a hooped tulle skirt and an intricately beaded bodice with a sweetheart neck, waved at everyone.

"Wow, the Peach Queen goes all out, doesn't she?" Georgie asked.

"Yeah. She looks like Cinderella before she turns into a pumpkin."

With a peal of laughter, Georgie said, "The coach turns into a pumpkin, silly. Not Cinderella."

He grinned. "Fairy tales aren't my thing. I was close."

Well, damn. He's even cuter with those dimples flashing.

"Oh, look at the kids on horseback," Georgie said, pointing to them. "Are they a 4-H club or something?"

"No, those are the nominees for the rodeo scholarship."

"What's a rodeo scholarship?"

"There's a formal on the twenty-first. Have you heard about it?"

"No, or if I did I forgot."

"It benefits the rodeo and funds a rodeo scholarship. It's not cheap entering rodeos, especially if you're intent on doing it professionally. The scholarship goes to a teenager who the committee picks every year."

"That sounds really nice. How do they decide who gets it?"

"I'm not sure. They say they have a method, but honestly, I think they throw names in a hat and pick one. You can only win it once."

"It sounds like fun."

"It is. Why don't you go with me?"

"I wasn't fishing for an invitation." Damn, the thought of going to an event like that, and with Spencer yet, was far too tempting.

"I didn't think you were. Neither of us is working. I checked. So how about it?"

He checked? Dang, there went that excuse. "I don't think that's a good idea."

"Why?"

"We work together."

"And?"

She didn't answer, preferring to ignore the question. She

went back to watching the parade. Maybe he'd give up if she didn't answer.

There was a float made like Santa's wonderland, with elves and toys, and a float decorated with a Christmas tree, with elves throwing candy to the waiting children as they passed. Santa came last in his "sleigh" pulled by horses. An old buggy had been converted to look like a sleigh and the horses sported reindeer horns tied to their heads.

"This is great," Georgie said. "I feel like a kid again. If only I had some candy."

"I can fix that." Spencer put his hand in his jacket pocket and pulled out a chocolate Christmas tree.

"Thanks. Do you want to share?" She didn't really want to but she thought she should be polite.

"No, you go ahead," he said with a chuckle.

She finished eating and wiped her hands on her jeans. Luckily they weren't too grubby. "Why are you looking at me like that?"

He reached out and wiped his thumb over the corner of her mouth. "You missed a spot."

His eyes had darkened. He looked like... He looked like he wanted to kiss her.

"I wish there was mistletoe up here."

Her stomach did a somersault. She'd been right. Damn Spencer. She'd done very well not thinking about that kiss. Okay, not well, but she'd managed for a little while. But now it all came rushing back. "Well, there's not."

"I know."

"We work together, Spencer."

"Yes, we do."

"Dating is not in the cards."

"Why?"

"Because I don't date coworkers."

"Why?"

She debated telling him and decided she might as well. "Workplace romances are a bad idea. Once burned twice shy."

"So you were burned."

"Yes."

"How do you know it was the working together that was the problem?"

"It wasn't a problem. At first. But as time went on it became one. After we broke up it was an even bigger problem. Seeing each other every day—" She broke off and shook her head. "I don't want to do that again." Sure, that hadn't been their only problem but it was one Georgie knew she could control. And working at the same place afterward had really sucked. For her, anyway.

He considered her for a little bit then said, "Okay."

"It's not you, Spencer," she added hastily.

"Okay. Don't worry about it. Let me know if you change your mind."

"Aren't you going to ask someone else?"

"Nope."

"Why?"

"Isn't it obvious? I want to go with you. If not you, I'll go stag."

A mother with two children—a baby and a four- or five-year-old—had come up to the rooftop a little while before. The baby began wailing while the older child tried to get the mom's attention too.

"She looks a little frazzled," Spencer said. He lifted an eyebrow at Georgie. "Want to help her out?"

She shouldn't have been surprised that Spencer's first thought had been to help. It was a shame he was a player. And even more that they'd be working together. "All right. Want me to take the baby?"

"Why? Think I can't handle a baby?"

"I didn't—"

"How terribly sexist of you. I wouldn't have thought it of you, Georgie."

She started to apologize but he was laughing. "I like babies," he said, and the next thing she knew Spencer had introduced both of them and had taken the baby from the mother and was entertaining him by making faces. He should have looked silly, but somehow, he didn't.

"You and your boyfriend saved my life," Tanya said. She had her son on her hip and Georgie pointed out things in the parade she thought he'd like.

"He's not my boyfriend. He's my coworker."

"Oh, sorry. You two seem so well suited."

Georgie laughed it off but she suffered a pang of regret. Lecturing herself on not needing a man to be happy didn't really help, either. Neither did reminding herself that her exboyfriend was every bit as charming as Spencer. But Cole had had a fatal flaw. He couldn't commit. Even after more than two years together, he *still* couldn't commit.

She hadn't demanded a marriage proposal, for God's sake. She'd simply wanted to know or feel that they were going somewhere, though, and not going on as they were forever.

By the time the parade wound down Tanya's husband had relieved Spencer of the baby and several other people had made their way to the rooftop. Georgie and Spencer went downstairs and had some of the cider Lilly had offered them earlier.

As she was getting ready to leave, Spencer asked, "What are you doing for the rest of the night?"

"I was planning on going to the tree lighting and Christkindlmarkt. Why?"

"Want to come a little early and help me pass out flyers for the toy drive at the market and the tree lighting?"

"Okay. You sure pass out a lot of flyers."

"Gotta advertise. I'll do it tomorrow too, at the Country Christmas Market. If you're not busy why don't you help me there?"

"Are we the only people who pass out these flyers?"

"Not by a long shot. I have friends in the neighboring communities and they're always happy to help out. I'll see you tonight. Say around five? The tree lighting is at six so that should leave us plenty of time."

He has enough energy for five people. I wonder if he ever slows down.

ONCE SHE RELAXED, Georgie discovered that Spencer was a lot of fun. She hadn't actually worked with him yet, other than on the toy drive, but they were both working Sunday and Monday and one of those days Spencer would be working with her as a paramedic.

But for now they'd finished passing out flyers to the crowd and were waiting for the lighting of the big tree in front of the library.

Spencer apparently knew everyone. And didn't have a problem flirting with all the women. And she meant *all* of the women. None of them seemed to mind, she noticed. Oddly enough, the men they were with didn't mind either. Which must mean it was harmless or the men saw it that way. She noticed that even though Spencer flirted, there was never any innuendo or anything offensive about it. And she was very critical when she watched him.

And why should she care if Spencer flirted? It made no difference to her, after all. *Keep telling yourself that.*

After passing flyers out to the crowd and while they waited for the tree-lighting ceremony to begin, she and Spencer ran across a little boy, probably around three, who was alone and crying. "Oh, he must be lost. Poor little thing."

She squatted down in front of him. He had curly blond hair and huge blue eyes, and his lashes and cheeks were wet with tears. "Are you lost? What's your name?"

He stuck his finger in his mouth and wouldn't answer. Spencer said, "That's Jeffrey Pierce." He picked him up and propped him on his hip. "Let's go find your mom, kiddo."

They hadn't gone far when a frazzled-looking woman,

holding a baby and towing a two-year-old along with her, rushed up. "Thank God. I turned around and he was gone. You're a lifesaver, Spencer."

He grinned and handed over the toddler. "That's my job. Where's Adam?"

"Working. And I hated for the kids to miss the tree lighting, but I should have known better than to try to bring them alone."

"Let us help," Spencer said. "Maybe the kids need some hot chocolate."

She threw him another grateful look. "If you're sure."

"Want chocolate," Jeffrey said.

"Me, me, me!" the little girl chimed in.

"Chocolate for both of you," Spencer said to the children before turning back to their mother. "I'll go get it. Why don't you stay here with Wanda and the kids, Georgie? That way you won't miss the lighting if it actually happens on time."

"You don't sound too sure that it will."

"In my experience it rarely does."

Jeffrey and the other toddler were tugging on their mom's clothes and demanding her attention. "Can I hold the baby while you see to Jeffrey and your little girl?" Georgie asked. "What are the girls' names?"

"Oh, thank you," she said, passing over the baby. "The baby's name is Brandy. And this," she said, motioning to the younger toddler, "is Becca." She squatted down to talk to both children, who settled down as soon as she did. She stood up, pressing a hand to her back. "Don't ask me why we decided to have our kids so close together."

"You do seem to have your hands full." Georgie jiggled the baby on her hip, which made her laugh and clap her hands.

"Bah," Brandy said, patting Georgie's cheek.

"That's the seal of approval," her mother said.

"Good to know," Georgie said with a laugh.

A little while later, Spencer came back with hot chocolate for all. As Spencer had warned, the lighting ceremony still hadn't started.

"Thanks," Georgie said, taking one. "You didn't need to bring me one."

"Do you like hot chocolate?"

"Of course. Who doesn't?"

"Never can tell. Anyway, drink up."

The weather was chilly, but not too cold. Georgie wore a sweater, jeans and a jacket. She noticed Spencer wore a leather bomber jacket. Damn, why did he look so good in everything? *It's just a jacket, you fool*, she lectured herself. *Are you going to drool over every little thing about the man?*

Probably.

The tree was huge and decorated with pine cones, garlands, bows and ornaments. A little before six-thirty Santa came and, with much fanfare and singing of Christmas carols, lit the tree. A collective gasp went up from the onlookers. What must have been at least a thousand twinkling lights of every color encircled the tree. A large golden star, also lighted, topped the tree. Once again Georgie marveled at how the town experienced Christmastime. They believed in going for it wholeheartedly.

Once the tree-lighting ceremony was over they left Wanda, who said she was taking her kids directly home. "I should go too," Georgie said.

"I'm going to my truck to pick up some flyers for the street vendors. Want to help me?"

"We aren't finished? I thought passing out the leaflets in the tree-lighting crowd was all we were doing."

"I'm not finished. You can be if you want."

"Of course I'll help you. You're tireless."

"No, I'm just a sucker for the kids."

"What about the older kids? Does anyone bring anything for them?"

"A couple of years ago we started something for the older kids. They fill out a paper ornament with what they want written on it and hang it up on a tree we put in the library. The community comes through for that as well."

"What happens if all the kids aren't picked?"

"That never happens. Everyone gets something."

"Spencer! You take the ones who are left, don't you?"

"No," he said frowning. Then he relented and said, "My family does. We all pitch in."

"You're really civic minded."

Spencer laughed and opened his truck door. "Nope. I just like kids and Christmas."

Georgie loved Christmas too. She and her family had always enjoyed the season. Cole, her ex, didn't exactly hate Christmas but she always had gotten the feeling he could take it or leave it. "Is the rest of your family like you?"

"You mean do they like Christmas?"

"Yes. And did they raise you to be so charitable? Are they all that way?"

Spencer gave her a curious look. "I never thought about that. It's just something we've always done. My mom was really poor growing up but her family always picked out an angel—a needy kid—from the Salvation Army giving tree. So we did too, from the time we were little. Now that we're all grown, we all do what we can to help."

He handed her a pile of flyers. "Let's go."

What a guy. If he wasn't such a flirt...and if I didn't work with him, I'd—

Yes, but he is and you do. Damn it.

SPENCER MCBRIDE KNEW everyone in town. It seemed that way, anyway. After taking care of the tree-lighting crowd, they took their flyers to the Christkindlmarkt and passed them out, not only to the vendors but to everyone they saw who would accept one. And to Georgie's surprise, most people took them. Sure, a lot of them tossed them almost immediately but Spencer seemed to think that enough people would remember and donate toys. They should, considering the entire town would be papered with flyers and posters about the toy drive.

This market was different from the market on Saturday and Sunday. The Friday evening market, which took place during and after the tree lighting, was a salute to the town's

German heritage. The name, Christkindlmarkt, was German and the wares were specialties such as those available in Germany at their markets. There was music, traditional German dances, and all kinds of food and drink. Candied, toasted almonds, traditional Christmas cookies like lebkuchen—a form of gingerbread. There was bratwurst, mulled wine, hot chocolate and various other goodies. There were booths with handmade Christmas ornaments and those with other handmade and carved items. The following two days the market would expand to have not only German traditions, but Texas ones as well, in a true country Christmas market.

Tonight the streetlights with their decorations were lit up, and so were the booths, many of them outlined in small, twinkling lights. It was crowded since not only the townspeople but also people from all over the area and some from far away attended.

Spencer had gone one way down Main Street and Georgie had taken the other. Once she ran out of flyers she went looking for Spencer. She got distracted by a booth showing off handmade, carved ornaments. Her apartment wasn't large, but it wasn't too small for a reasonably sized Christmas tree and she wanted a tree for her first Christmas in her new home. She'd just finished paying for several ornaments when she turned around and almost ran into Spencer.

"I ran out of flyers," she said before he could speak.

"I figured. You don't need to apologize for enjoying the market. That's what it's here for."

"I didn't want you to think I was shirking my duties."

He laughed. "Don't worry, I didn't. Besides, it's voluntary. You're not ready to go home, are you? Let's go watch the dancers."

"Dancers?"

"Yeah, there's a group who perform some original German dances. That's tonight. Tomorrow Creekbend High School will have some dancers."

"Okay, sounds fun."

"There are handcrafted beers and some of the wineries will have booths too."

So they watched dancers, drank handcrafted beer and ate stollen, a German fruit bread with nuts, spices and icing. After that they strolled down to the Catholic church to see the lighted Nativity scene on the front lawn.

"It looks like they're starting to close down," Georgie said, conscious of a wish that the night could continue. Spencer was a lot of fun. Plus, she didn't feel guilty that she was breaking her rule against dating coworkers since this clearly wasn't a date. No, they were just hanging together.

"Want to go have a drink at the Saloon?" Spencer asked.

"No, thanks. I'm about to pop. It's a good thing I walked here."

"You walked?"

"I only live a few blocks away. At the Peachtree apartments."

He grinned. "What a coincidence."

"What do you mean?"

"I live at the Peachtree too."

"You live at—"

"At the Peachtree apartments," he finished for her. "It's not really surprising, Georgie. A lot of people who work at the hospital or fire department live there. They're close and far more affordable than the Millennial Village," he said, naming the newer, and more expensive, high-rise condos directly across from the hospital.

"You have your truck here."

He shrugged. "I can either drive you or walk you home and come back for it. It's a nice night. I wouldn't mind the walk."

She couldn't say no without seeming rude. And silly. Besides, hadn't she just thought she didn't want the evening to end? "Okay, if you're sure." Another thought occurred to her, having lived in the city all her life. "There's not a lot of crime here, is there?"

"No, why? Is that why you thought I wanted to walk you home?"

"The thought crossed my mind. I came from Houston, remember?"

"You can relax. Shane Highwater, Last Stand's police chief, wouldn't tolerate anything like that. Last Stand is one of the safest places there is."

"Oh, good. I noticed a lot of people don't even lock doors. I lock everything. It's a habit."

"It's a good habit to have. Bad things can happen even in the safest of towns."

"Better paranoid than sorry?"

"Exactly," he answered with a grin.

Chapter Five

THE LAST STAND Country Christmas Market was one of the town's biggest events. Food was one of the main attractions and was everywhere to be found. In the streets were all sorts of vendors' booths. The shop doors were all thrown open, welcoming customers inside. There were Christmas candies from the candy store, pies from Char-Pie, German bakery specialties from Kolaches, hot cider, hot chocolate, bratwurst, buffalo wings, cookies, cakes and other specialties from the restaurants and bakeries. There were lots of things to buy: Texas memorabilia, crafts of all kinds, from handmade carved wooden bric-a-brac to quilts, hand-knitted blankets and sweaters. There was even a specialty shop that made dog biscuits. He never knew exactly how many dogs would be living on the ranch, but he always bought a large bucket for Jessie to distribute among them.

The market was a big deal and an annual event, so vendors came from all around the area and some as far away as Austin or San Antonio. And of course, there were toys out the wazoo. Cowboy hats and western wear, and Kelly Boots from Whiskey River hosted a booth with their famous custom-made cowboy boots.

Spencer had asked Georgie to come out Saturday morning to help him distribute more flyers. He thought the campaign was working well because it seemed like the barrels had been fuller than they were last year at the same time of the drive. But maybe that was wishful thinking.

Speaking of that, he almost wished he didn't work with Georgie. She'd been adamant that she didn't want to date a coworker. But he hadn't given up trying to change her mind. They were working together for the next shift, so at least that would give him time to talk to her and maybe find out exactly what had happened to make her so gun-shy. She'd already said she'd been burned. But she hadn't mentioned what had actually happened.

He and Georgie went in opposite directions and met back when they'd passed out all their leaflets. "Have you eaten?" he asked her.

"No. But I'm going to. I just don't know what I want."

"Depends on whether you want lunch food or sweets."

She put her finger to her lips, miming thinking. "Both."

"Okay, there's a booth with the best bratwurst you ever tasted."

"Lead on."

So they ate brats, chicken wings, corn on the cob and latkes. Then they moved on to the sweets. There were cookies made in traditional Christmas shapes, and stollen. There were all kinds of candies and candied fruits. He and Georgie split a number of items, since they'd have foundered if they each ate a serving of everything they saw.

"Have you eaten at Char-Pie yet?" Spencer asked.

"I haven't been in, but I had a piece last week when someone brought it to work. It was delicious."

"Come with me, then. Charlie, the owner, is my brother Turner's girlfriend. Her pies are great."

He introduced Georgie to Charlie and her sister Audrey, thinking the sisters might be nice friends for her to have. Plus Charlie and Audrey both had a soft spot for him so they'd say nice things about him. At least, he hoped they would.

Why? It's not like you're gonna go out with her.

Never say never.

Charlie was busy so couldn't talk much but Audrey managed to talk to Georgie in between customers. While he was talking to a friend he noticed the two women exchanged phone numbers.

"We'll get out of your way," Georgie said.

"Okay, I'll call you with a couple of dates and you can pick which one works for you."

"Sounds good."

"It looked like you and Audrey hit it off," Spencer said after they found a place to stand and eat their pie. There wasn't a hope of finding a table since the shop was teeming with people.

Georgie forked a bite of pecan pie into her mouth. "Oh my God, this is so good." She ate some more then said, "Sorry. I was having a moment with my pie. Yes, we did. She wants to arrange a girls' night with some friends and introduce me around. She says I just missed the first Wednesday girls' night out."

"My sister Jessie goes to that. It's on the first Wednesday of the month. I hear they get wild and crazy," he said, teasingly.

"They do?"

He laughed. "I don't think so, but they have a good time. They always end it at the Last Stand Saloon. Have you been there yet?"

"No, but I heard a little about the legend."

"The legend? You mean how Last Stand got its name?" She nodded. "That's no legend. It's the truth. What did you hear?"

"Something about the Texas Revolution and the Mexican army. I think I heard there was some kind of standoff."

"Let me tell you the real story. Last Stand was a wide spot in the road during the Texas Revolution. The Mexican army under Santa Anna—you know, the general who massacred the people at the Alamo—they came through here figuring they'd squash us like bugs, but a handful of men, women and children holed up in the Saloon, which was the sturdiest building in town, and held them off. The bullet holes from that battle are still in the walls. It was the Texians' last stand, hence the name."

"Texians? Don't you mean Texans?"

"Have you forgotten your Texas history? Back then they were called Texians."

"I stand corrected. I had forgotten that. My course on Texas history was a long time ago. How do you know the story is true?"

"Besides the bullet holes in the Saloon walls? We've got

journals from the people who fought. Ones who died and ones who lived to tell the whole story. History books, that sort of thing. The library has all that information in a special room. They've got a lot of Texas history and journals and things like that. You can't check them out of the library but you can read them there."

"I'll have to look into that. Has your family been here that long?"

"Absolutely. Old Doc McBride was one of the original settlers."

"You really do come from a medical family, don't you?"

"I do. But I'm the rebel," he said and winked at her.

"Seems to me your sister is more of a rebel than you. You're in the medical profession, after all."

"Yes, but I'm not a doctor."

She looked at him curiously. "Does it bother you not to be a doctor?"

"No. I know what it took for my brothers to become doctors. Not for me. But what I do now? Firefighting and medicine? That's the best of both worlds."

❦

"I NEED A wheelbarrow to roll me around," Georgie said as they left the pie shop.

"We'll walk. You'll feel better after that. You did kind of pack it away."

She stopped and stared at him. "What?"

He chuckled. "You should see your face. Just kidding.

You didn't eat that much."

"Yes, I did. But it was rude of you to notice." Her lips twitched when she said it. "I have a fast metabolism."

"Good to know."

They went back to the street and Georgie bought some Christmas ornaments. Spencer didn't buy anything but he enjoyed watching Georgie experience Last Stand at Christmas. They were standing beside a booth when someone ran into Georgie, pushing her into him. He put his arm around her to steady her. "You okay?"

"Yes. Sorry about that."

He wasn't. He looked up and grinned. "Well, well. Look what we're standing under."

She looked up and frowned. "You did that on purpose. You knew there was mistletoe at this booth."

"No I didn't."

"Right," she said drawing the word out. "It's not happening, Spencer." She moved away from him.

He shrugged. "Can't blame a guy for trying." He tilted his head, considering her. "Relax, Georgie. I'm kidding."

"I know you think it's not a big deal but—"

He held up a hand to stop her. "I know. You don't date coworkers. Which means you don't kiss them either." Which was, in his opinion, a damn shame.

"Exactly."

He spotted old man Appleblum waving at him. "Come on, I'll introduce you to someone."

Fred Appleblum wasn't as old as Last Stand's matriarch, Minna Herdmann, but he ran a close second. Spencer introduced him to Georgie.

"Nice to meet you, Gigi. Where have you been hiding her, Spencer?"

Fred was deaf as a post and though he wore his hearing aids, more often than not he forgot to put new batteries in. "Georgie, not Gigi," he said loudly. "She's new in town." He extended his hand, palm up. "Hand 'em over."

"I just changed the batteries," Fred said indignantly.

Spencer continued to hold out his hand. Fred took his hearing aids out and put them in his palm, then looked in his pockets until he came up with a pack of the tiny batteries. He could see Georgie, biting her lip and trying not to laugh. "Get these new batteries out for me," he told her. "You might as well do something useful."

Grinning, she did as he said, handing him a new battery as he exchanged each dead one with her. Honestly, he wasn't sure how Fred—with his gnarled, arthritic fingers—managed to manipulate those tiny round discs anyway.

Batteries replaced, he handed the hearing aids and the battery pack back to the old man. Fred stuck the batteries back in his pocket and returned his hearing aids to his ears.

"Where's Honor, Fred?"

"Danged if you weren't right," he said, patting an ear. "Honor? She went to get me something but damned if I can remember what. Are we on for Tuesday afternoon?"

"Sure but I can't play long. You know I'm in charge of the toy drive."

"You always are," Fred said. To Georgie he added, "Boy pretends it's a chore but you can tell he likes it."

They arranged to meet in their usual place, the park, unless it rained and then they went to Char-Pie or the library. Fred's daughter, Honor, came back a few moments later and handed Fred a funnel cake. Spencer introduced the two women and then they left.

"I want a funnel cake," Georgie said. "But I'm way too full."

"It's not the kind of thing you save until later. But you never got any gingerbread. That will keep."

"Okay, you talked me into it."

"Coming right up." They started walking toward the booth, which was at the other end of the market. As they walked, Georgie looked at him quizzically.

"What?"

"Is Fred a relative of yours?"

"No, why?"

"You treated him like he was your grandpa. And what did he mean, are we on for Tuesday?"

"No, we're not related. Fred was one of my dad's patients. I've known him forever."

When he didn't elaborate she asked, "What happens on Tuesday?"

"Unless I'm working, we play dominoes in the park every Tuesday." He shot her a quick grin and added, "Sometimes we get really wild and play checkers instead."

"That's awfully sweet of you."

He shifted uncomfortably at the admiration in her gaze. "That's me. Sweet as apple pie. Besides, Fred is a chick magnet."

Georgie laughed. "How devious of you."

"You just said I was sweet."

"I take it back. Seriously, Spencer, doesn't he have other people he can play with?"

"Well, sure, but he plays with them all the time. He likes to play with me. Says it challenges him."

"Does it?"

"Hell, no. He's a crafty old guy. Beats me regularly." She had that look on her face again. "It's not a big deal."

"Maybe not to you, but it clearly is to him."

"Here's the gingerbread booth," he said, glad for the change of subject. To be honest, he got as much of a kick out of their weekly game as Fred did. Fred was never at a loss for a story about one of the town's citizens, or about Last Stand back in the day.

Spencer had to squelch the automatic offer to pay for Georgie's cake. He suspected she would tell him she was perfectly capable of buying her own food. Besides, it wasn't like they were on a date. After he checked with the guy running the booth to be certain he had enough flyers for the toy drive, Georgie said she was going home.

He didn't want her to leave. Sure, they'd been there all day but he hated to see it end. Damn, you'd think he was falling for the woman.

Aren't you?

No. It's too soon. I haven't even known her a week.

What difference does that make?

"Spencer? Why are you staring at me like that?"

"I was thinking about something else. But now that you

mention it, you have powdered sugar on your face."

"I do not. You made that up. I ate the stollen much earlier." At his grin she said, "Oh, my God. You let me wander all over the place with food on my face?"

"It's only a little dab." He wiped it off with his thumb. She was so close. Her eyes were a clear blue, like a cloudless sky. He wanted to kiss her. To find out if that kiss under the mistletoe had been a fluke. But he didn't. Regretfully, he knew they had a ways to go before she'd be ready for that.

She might never be ready. What will you do then?

Damn, don't be such a killjoy.

It's my job.

Sometimes his alter ego really pissed him off.

SUNDAY WAS GEORGIE'S first day to work with Spencer. Their first call was to a "sick person" midway through the morning. It turned out to be a middle-aged woman who had a fever of a hundred and one and insisted she needed to be transported to the emergency room. They checked her over, took her vitals, including her temperature, to find it was only ninety-nine. The rest of her vitals were normal as well. Spencer was able to talk her out of going to the ER by convincing her to call her doctor first thing in the morning.

"Exciting first call, huh?" Spencer asked her once they were back in the ambulance.

Georgie laughed. "Do you get a lot like that? That was one of our common ones where I worked in Houston."

"Not too bad. A lot of them either drive themselves to the ER or get a relative or friend to drive them. Some even wait and go to their own doctor."

"Bless those people. You were very patient with her."

Spencer shot her a surprised look. "No one likes a cranky paramedic."

"True." But she'd worked with one or two who weren't nearly as patient as he'd been.

When they got back to the station, Georgie made a bunch of sandwiches for several of the crew. They'd just sat down when the tones came. Tones were what most paramedics called the warning ding they received before a radio message from the dispatcher. Unsurprisingly, this was just like her old job. Paramedics and firefighters rarely had a chance to finish a meal. She stuffed half the sandwich in her mouth and took the rest with her to eat on the way.

This call was also someone feeling sick. However, this time the patient really was sick. "What's your name, ma'am?" Georgie asked her upon arrival.

"Mary," she said. "I feel awful. I tested my blood and my sugar is high."

"Are you diabetic, Mary?" Spencer asked.

"Well, of course," she said, staring at him. "I just told you my sugar is high."

"We have to ask, Mary, just to be sure," Georgie said. "What was your blood glucose level?"

"Three hundred, I think."

They performed another glucose test, pricking her finger and testing her blood. "You're right, it's a little high,"

Spencer said to Mary. "Let's get you to the hospital."

He exchanged a meaningful look with Georgie. A glucose level of higher than 240 warranted a trip to the hospital. One of 350, what Mary's test just showed, meant they needed to transport her immediately. But the patient probably knew that as well as they did. Fortunately they were able to get her to the hospital quickly so she could be treated.

Nothing was happening back at the fire station so they sat down to watch TV in the room off the kitchen. It was full of comfy chairs, a couple of couches, and a coffee table that was just the right height to put your feet up on. Georgie and Spencer both sat on the couch. She picked up the remote first, smiling to herself when she noticed Spencer was looking between the remote and the TV. "Let me guess," Georgie said. "You have to be in charge of the flipper."

"Not at all," he said loftily.

She changed channels until she found one she liked, and was fairly sure Spencer wouldn't. It was a show on HGTV about fixing up old houses. She moved around until she was comfortable with her legs tucked up beside her.

"That's what you decided on?" Spencer asked.

"Yes. Why, don't you like it?"

"No, I don't. Besides, you don't even have a house. You live in an apartment."

"True, but I won't forever. Someday I'll have a house and I'll need to know how to do this stuff."

He shrugged. "Whatever blows your skirt up."

"Cute. But I'm not wearing a dress. I'm wearing pants. Whatever sizzles your bacon."

"There's no bacon here. Whatever butters your toast."

"Whatever peels your banana."

"Whatever floats your boat."

"Whatever floats your goat."

Spencer held up a hand, laughing. "Stop. We could go on forever like this."

She laughed too. "You started it." She took pity on him, handing him the remote. "Here, you take it. You're clearly frustrated."

"Thanks. And yes, I was."

At least he admitted it, she thought with another smile. Georgie watched him flip through channels, finally settling on a basketball game between two teams she had zero interest in. "What happens when you have to deal with someone else who's a control freak?"

He frowned at her before returning to the game. "I'm not a control freak. Just because I like to drive and like to control the remote doesn't mean I'm obsessive about it."

She lifted an eyebrow. "Really?"

"Okay," he conceded. "So I'm a little bit of a control freak. But I'm fine with things I have no control over. Like work. We never know what's going to happen. Whether the shift will be boring as hell, or interesting, or terrible, or a mix of all three."

"True. I'd think that would bother you."

"I like it. Unless it's a really bad day. But no one likes those."

Spencer intrigued her. Was there more to the straight-forward guy he seemed to be? She still thought that control issues didn't go well with their profession, where so much was out of your control, but he obviously made it work. She'd heard nothing but good things about him since she'd arrived. His coworkers and everyone else she'd talked to thought he was a stand-up guy. Sure, he flirted and dated a lot but that was no surprise. He was young—he hadn't hit thirty yet—single and a firefighter. Women had probably been throwing themselves at him since he came back to town, if not before that.

Why was she so curious about Spencer's private life when she had no intention of dating him?

Chapter Six

FAMILIES WERE A pain in the ass. Once a month Spencer's entire family, or everyone who wasn't sick, working, or willing to face their sister Jessie's wrath, was expected to be there. Spencer usually enjoyed it but tonight they all decided to rag on him about Georgie Durant. The same Georgie Durant who'd been definite that she didn't date coworkers, and she didn't intend to change her mind anytime soon. Damn it.

The night had started like it always did. Tonight the entire family: his mother, his father, Jessie, Graham and his wife Bella—who were annoyingly madly in love—Turner and his girlfriend Charlie—also crazy in love—and Spencer himself had all managed to make it. His mom, Rita, had made her famous chili and then they'd all settled in for a few hands of poker and beer.

"Who's the pretty redhead you were all over at the Corbyns' party, Spencer?" Turner asked.

Spencer shot him an irritated look. "I kissed her under the mistletoe. That's not the definition of being all over someone."

Turner shrugged. "Potato, potah-toe. It looked pretty

intense to me. Raise you ten, and call," he said.

"Fold," Charlie said. "She's a new paramedic in town. She's been into the pie shop a few times already. I like her."

"You like everyone who buys your pie," Spencer returned.

"Yeah, so?" she said, and everyone laughed. "Audrey set up a girls' night out for her on Thursday."

"Didn't you already have first Wednesday?" Spencer asked, referring to the women's traditional girls' night out on the first Wednesday of every month.

"Yes. Last Wednesday. But we can meet more than once a month if we want."

"Cards on the table," their mom said, laying down three kings to go with the one on the table.

Typical. Either his mom or Jessie won more than their fair share of hands. "Damn, Mom. Your luck is outrageous."

"Skill, my boy. It's skill more than luck," she chided him. "Tell me about this new woman. Are you dating her yet?"

"Inquiring minds want to know," Jessie added. "I saw you two together at the Christmas market. And you told me you wanted to date her."

"And you were with her at the tree lighting too," his sister-in-law Bella added.

Women—especially women family members—were a royal pain in the ass at times. In Last Stand gossip ran like the Pedernales River. "She's working on the toy drive with me. It's no big deal and we're not dating."

"But you want to," Graham said. "What's up with that?"

Exasperated, Spencer looked at his dad. "Don't look at me," Tommy McBride said. "I'm staying out of it."

"Well, that's one of you." He turned back to the others. "She doesn't date coworkers. Period. End of story."

"Isn't it hard working with her when you have a thing for her and she won't go out with you?" Jessie speculated.

Spencer set his jaw. "Good God, Jessie. I just met the woman. I do not have a thing for her." And that, he admitted silently, was a stinking lie.

"He's cranky," Jessie said to Bella. "Always a sign."

Bella nodded sagely. "Every time."

"Can we get back to poker? You know, the reason we're here?"

"We can but Bella and I have something to say," Graham said.

Spencer had noticed Bella was drinking water instead of a beer, so he wasn't terribly surprised when Graham said, "Bella's pregnant."

Everyone started congratulating, hugging, and talking at once. The two had only gotten married in October. "That was fast," Turner said. "Is Graham's biological clock ticking?"

Graham looked at Turner and rubbed his cheek with his middle finger, which made everyone laugh. He was a good bit older than Bella, but he wasn't terribly sensitive about it. Which was a good thing, considering how much their family liked to give people a hard time.

"We think it happened on our honeymoon," Bella said. "We weren't planning to start a family so soon but the kid seems to have a mind of his own."

"You already know the sex?"

"No, but I think it's a boy. Graham says it's a girl."

"We need to get a pool going," Turner said. "What's the due date so we can have an idea?"

"You are not having a betting pool on our baby," Bella said.

"Why not?" Spencer asked. "You know the entire staff at the hospital will. You don't want the family to miss out, do you?"

Jessie laughed. "You might as well give in, Bella. We're just going to do it anyway."

"Do you people bet on everything?"

"Just poker and baby pools. Well, sports too, of course."

"Of course," she agreed. "Well, since I can't stop you maybe I should join you."

"Foul," Turner said. "The mom and dad don't get to bet."

"That seems unfair. What do you think, Graham?"

"Let them have their fun, Bella. After all, we're the ones who get the baby."

Everyone laughed.

Spencer wondered what it would be like to be as crazy in love with a woman as his brothers were. He never had been. He'd been busy with his career and enjoying himself too much to worry about settling down. But then he met Georgie and suddenly being involved with one woman seemed a lot more attractive than it had been in the past.

Too bad she wouldn't even go on a date with him.

AUDREY CALLED GEORGIE a couple of days after they met to arrange for a day that was good for Georgie to meet with her and some friends. They settled on Thursday, at the Saloon. Audrey also told her to invite whoever she wanted. She asked Marcella since she was one of the few people she felt like she knew. Marcella told her she sometimes went to First Wednesday so she would probably know most of the women that Audrey asked, but she wasn't close friends with any of them.

Besides being the site of the battle for which the town was named during the Texas Revolution, the bar was also well-known for having no TVs. Slater Highwater, the owner, refused to have any in the place. But there was a jukebox, a pool table, good drinks and snack food, so no one missed the blare of a TV. There were several places around town where you could watch sports and drink if that was your thing.

Georgie arrived a bit early and Marcella was the only other person there. Her friend already had a beer in front of her. "I hope it's not a bad sign that we're the only two here," Georgie said.

"We're early. I'm sure they'll be here soon."

"I'm going to get a beer."

When she came back Marcella asked, "So, how is it—working with Spencer?"

She sipped her beer and put it down. "He's great to work with. Professional. Good at what he does." But she still couldn't figure him out. Just when she saw him flirting with a woman and decided he was incorrigible, he'd do something nice. Like at the tree lighting when he'd helped his friend with her kids. Or finding out he apparently spent every Tuesday playing games with an old man.

"Is that all?"

Georgie shrugged. "Can I ask you something?"

"Sure."

"Is Spencer McBride for real?"

Marcella stopped with her beer halfway to her mouth. "What do you mean? For real in what way?"

Georgie told her about being at the market with him and what he'd done. "I mean, he flirts with women but they like it. He's not offensive about it. And the guys like him. You can tell."

"Yes, you can. Everyone—well, almost everyone—likes Spencer. He's a likeable guy. And this is a bad thing?"

She drank some beer. "No, of course not. But he seems too good to be true."

"Well, he's not perfect. He doesn't ever date a woman for long."

"Hell, you can say that about half the single men in town. Maybe more."

"You have a point. I went out with him a couple of times."

"You did? What happened?"

"Nothing. Well, nothing much."

"Meaning what? Did you—" Georgie stopped herself. What Marcella did or didn't do in the past was none of her business. "Sorry, just ignore me. I didn't mean to pry."

"No, we didn't sleep together," Marcella said, answering Georgie's unasked question with a quick smile. "I was tempted, though."

"Why didn't you?"

"I saw my ex-boyfriend when we were at dinner and since I was still sort of hung up on him, it spoiled the mood."

"Do I know your ex?" Georgie asked.

"Yes, it's Cable. It doesn't matter what I do, I just can't completely get over him. I wish I could."

Georgie nodded sympathetically and then drank some beer. "I had to move to another city to get over mine."

"You moved away completely? Was he that bad?"

"No, damn it. He was that good. But he couldn't, or wouldn't commit. All I wanted was to know that we were going somewhere, you know? I finally got tired of it and realized he was never going to change. So I broke it off. After a couple of months of seeing him all the time—because we worked together—I decided to move."

"That's pretty drastic. Are you glad you did?"

"I am. It's been good, not having to see him constantly. I feel like I'm finally over him."

"Must be nice," Marcella muttered. "Is that why you won't give Spencer a chance? Because you work with him?"

"That's right. After Cole and I split I decided I wouldn't date a coworker again."

"What if Spencer wasn't a coworker?"

"If he wasn't a coworker I'd be tempted. But he is."

"So you are tempted."

"Honestly, who wouldn't be tempted? But I'm not getting burned like that again. It's just too hard if things don't work out." They both drank some beer and Georgie asked, "Just out of curiosity, who doesn't like Spencer?"

"One person. That I know of, anyway. Brent Meyers got drunk and started slapping around his girlfriend—in public, yet. Spencer was there and didn't take kindly to it. He kicked Brent's ass. And I mean, really kicked his ass. So of course, Brent doesn't like him."

"I can see Spencer doing that." Very much in keeping with what she knew of his personality.

Audrey and Charlie came in just then and shortly after that, several other women showed up. So that was the end of any private conversation with Marcella.

"Everyone, this is Georgie," Audrey said. "She's a new paramedic in town. She just moved here a couple of weeks ago." Everyone introduced themselves. There were five other women besides Marcella, Audrey and Georgie. Georgie was certain she wouldn't remember all of them. But as she talked to each of them and got to know them a little better she decided there was a chance she might keep them straight.

Sage Highwater raised and trained reining horses, which Georgie thought was fascinating. Sage had three brothers. Georgie had already met all three: Shane, the police chief; Sean, a Last Stand detective; and of course, Slater, who owned the bar.

"Do you ride, Georgie?" Sage asked.

"No. I wouldn't mind trying but I've never been on a horse. I petted one once, though."

Sage and Spencer's sister Jessie laughed. "We'll have to take her riding. Jessie raises and rescues mustangs," Sage added, before turning aside to talk to one of the other women.

"Spencer told me you did," Georgie said to Jessie. "He said you've been in love with mustangs since you were a little girl."

"Very true." Jessie smiled and drank some beer. "I thought for a while that Spencer would break tradition and help me raise horses but it didn't happen."

"I've only worked with him once so far, but he's very good at what he does."

"All my brothers are," Jessie said. "They all pitch in when I need help. Spencer is especially good about it." She drank more beer, then said, "But don't you dare tell him I said that."

Georgie laughed. "I promise I won't."

"Sometimes I wish that one of them was interested in ranching or raising horses," Jessie continued. "But it's probably best that they aren't."

"Why is that?" Georgie asked curiously.

"I like to be the boss," she said simply.

"I can vouch for that," Sage said. "When we were kids, we finally had to make a strict schedule of whose turn it was to run things."

All three of them laughed. Georgie looked forward to getting to know them better. They were a lot of fun.

She talked to Audrey for a while and really liked her. "Can I ask you something?" Georgie said.

"Sure. Ask me anything. Well, almost anything," she amended.

"Can you get a tan?"

Audrey burst out laughing. "Are you kidding? I'm a natural redhead. I have to slather on sunscreen to walk outside."

"Me too! It's so annoying. In high school everyone would lie out to get a tan and I'd have to hide in the shade."

Georgie and Audrey bonded over their shared hair color among other things that interested each of them. Georgie also had time to talk more in depth to both Jessie and Sage about their respective horse-raising operations. There were a few of the women she only said hello to, but she'd been invited to join the "First Wednesday" group of women so she knew she'd eventually get to know everyone.

Chapter Seven

TOWARD EVENING OF their twenty-four-hour shift, Georgie and Spencer had an emergency at the Caldwell ranch.

"Good Lord where is this place?" Georgie asked after they'd been driving for what seemed like hours. It hadn't really been hours, but they'd been driving for at least half an hour and it seemed like longer. "I had no idea there was so much undeveloped land around Last Stand."

"Yeah, the Caldwell place is pretty far outside of town."

"So you've been here before?"

He nodded. "One of the ranch hands fell off a ladder and we got called in. No idea what he was doing on that ladder but he broke his leg. Nasty break, too."

"Did they say who called this one in?"

"From what the dispatcher said, it sounded like Jethro's granddaughter, Gretchen, was with him and called it in. She's about fourteen and a very level-headed kid. She wouldn't have called us out for nothing. And I know Jethro, and I do, he's going to pitch a fit when he sees us. He 'don't believe in doctors and such.'"

She couldn't help smiling. "I take it we're the 'and

such.'"

Spencer shot her a grin. "Yep." He was driving, which she'd already discovered he did every time he possibly could.

At first she'd wondered if he was one of *those* men. The ones who refused to let a woman drive. But from what she heard at the station, he liked to drive no matter who was with him. She'd managed to get there ahead of him a couple of times and take the driver's seat. The first time he'd looked at her and said, "I don't suppose—"

"Don't even think it," she'd responded. After that she noticed he always tried to get to the ambulance before her. It had become something of a race to see who arrived first and drove. Strangely enough, he didn't insist on driving when they had a patient. In that case they rotated who took care of the patient and who drove.

"Why are you so insistent on driving?" she asked.

"I'm not."

"Of course you are."

"Most people don't fight about who drives."

"Seriously, Spencer, are you simply a control freak or is there another reason?"

Frowning, he glanced at her. "No one has ever asked me that before."

"So there is a reason."

He shrugged. "There's a reason."

She waited. He sent her another glance, this time a measured one. "I worked in Dallas for about a year and a half, when I first got my certification. We were called to an emergency and some fool blew through a stop sign and broadsided us. Siren shrieking and all. I was riding shotgun. If I'd been driving I'm pretty sure we could have avoided the wreck."

"So your driver screwed up?"

"Not exactly. I just don't think he reacted as quickly as he could have."

"Was anyone hurt?"

"My partner broke his arm and I cracked a couple of ribs. Luckily we hadn't picked up the patient yet. The driver of the SUV that hit us didn't have a scratch on him, naturally. Ever since then I prefer to drive."

"I think I would too. But you don't insist when we have a patient."

"That's because I'm too busy with the patient to worry."

She'd definitely heard worse reasons. "I won't try to drive anymore."

"Yes, you will. I know it's irrational and I need to cede control. At least sometimes. Besides, you're a good driver."

She laughed. "Thank you."

It began to rain, but not heavily. Georgie thought they were going to be on the highway forever. Finally, they turned off but then drove over an endless dirt and gravel road. They had to stop and open and close fence gates with cattle guards several times. They drove across gullies, ditches, and up and down hills. The state of the road was passable so far, but she suspected if it rained too much more getting out would be next to impossible. "Do the Caldwells drive this route every time they need to go somewhere?"

"Only way in, only way out."

"Good Lord, they must have to start forty-five minutes early to get anywhere on time."

"It's only Jethro and the ranch hands most of the time, unless his daughter or granddaughter are visiting."

"I don't think I'd deal with living out here very well."

"The McBride ranch is remote enough for me."

"It's not. From the way you and Jessie talk about it, it doesn't sound remote."

"Exactly."

Still smiling, she saw a simple limestone and wood farmhouse come into view. A young girl holding an umbrella, who had apparently been waiting for them, greeted them. "Thanks for coming. Grandpa doesn't know I called you but he's still bleeding and I'm worried."

"Happy to help, Gretchen," Spencer said.

"How long ago did the accident happen?" Georgie asked.

"Maybe an hour. Maybe more. I didn't really notice because I was trying to hurry back with some towels and didn't want Grandpa to know I was calling 9-1-1."

"Where is Jethro?" Spencer asked.

"He's in the barn. He was carving a Nativity scene and jammed a tool into his hand."

When they reached the barn, Gretchen opened a door to a small room filled with all kinds of carved wooden items. In the middle of the room, with a bloody piece of fabric tied around his hand, sat Jethro Caldwell. He was the epitome of an old Texas rancher, wearing boots, jeans, a long-sleeved western shirt, and a battered cowboy hat. Though it chilly in the barn, he didn't wear a coat.

"Did you bring me another towel?" Jethro asked and then his expression changed when he saw the two of them. "What the heck? What's EMS doing here? Gretchen, dang it, I told you not to call anyone."

"I'm sorry, Grandpa, but I didn't want you bleeding to death on my watch."

"I'm not bleeding to death. I've almost got it staunched. And since when do you have to watch me, girlie?"

"Since Mom told me to make sure you didn't hurt yourself carving. Which you did."

Georgie hid a smile. Jethro's granddaughter clearly had no fear of either her grandfather's crankiness or of standing up to him when necessary.

"Hi, Jethro," Spencer said. "Since we're here, how about letting us take a look at your hand? This is my new partner, Georgie Durant."

He grunted. Georgie couldn't tell what that meant but she said, "Nice to meet you, Mr. Caldwell."

"You're a pretty girl," the old man told her, "but I don't hold with doctors and such. Even pretty ones."

"Thank you," Georgie said, "but I'm afraid we still have to look at your hand."

"Since we're here—" Spencer began again.

Clearly impatient, Jethro interrupted. "If I let you look will you go away?"

"Eventually." He exchanged a significant look with Georgie, which she took to mean the less said about taking him to the hospital the better.

"What happened to Gretchen? That child is gonna get a

piece of my mind."

The wind had picked up as well as the rain. "I imagine she's gone into the house. Your accident really shook her, Jethro."

Jethro snorted. "We'd better go into the house as well, before the storm gets worse." He went over to a pegboard and looked at his coat, but since he was still holding the rag on his hand, he couldn't pick it up. Spencer took it off the hook and put it around Jethro's shoulders. He grunted what Georgie supposed was a thanks.

Once inside the farmhouse, Georgie and Spencer managed to get the old man to let them clean his wound but he refused to let them transport him to the hospital. Spencer, Georgie, and Gretchen all tried but Jethro wouldn't budge.

Finally, Spencer said, "You really need a couple of stitches but if you won't go, you won't. We'll Steri-Strip it, but you're going to have to be careful not to tear open the wound. These wound closure strips don't always hold, especially with this one being on your hand. However," Spencer added as Georgie put the thin strips of tape over the gouge in his hand, "I'm not leaving until you promise you'll go see your doctor tomorrow."

Gretchen had returned by then. "I'll tell Mom. Don't worry, he'll go."

"Damn interfering women," he muttered. "Always after a man to do something he doesn't need to do."

Georgie had thought his comment might hurt his grand-daughter's feelings but she was made of stronger stuff than that.

"More something you don't *want* to do, Grandpa. But don't worry. Mom and I will take care of you."

"Hmph. That's what I'm afraid of." But he smiled at Gretchen affectionately when he said it.

🖂

"IS JETHRO TYPICAL of ranchers around here?" Georgie asked as they drove away. "He doesn't seem to have much use for the medical profession."

Spencer glanced at her. "Well, he's not atypical. Most of them, especially the old-timers, think they can handle anything but the worst accident. Broken bones—if they're bad enough, heart attacks, chainsaw accidents and other similar injuries are worth calling it in. Pretty much everything else is considered minor."

Spencer didn't tell Georgie, but he was a little concerned that they might get stuck somewhere on the way back to the highway. The Caldwells' "road" was little better than a dirt track at times and with the rain increasing steadily since they arrived, there would be some tricky spots.

"Do you think he'll go see the doctor tomorrow?"

"You heard Gretchen. She and her mom are a force to be reckoned with."

Georgie laughed. "I can't see him being afraid of anything."

"Oh, he's not afraid. He just knows it's in his best interest to do what those two want."

"The rain is getting worse," she commented after a minute. "How you can see a thing is beyond me."

"Luckily I'm familiar with the road." Otherwise he'd have gotten off course long before this.

"How much longer until we get to the highway? We left at least half an hour ago."

Spencer glanced at her and saw she was serious. "You really are a city girl, aren't you?"

"Yes, but why do you say that?"

"There's no way I can tell how long it will take in these conditions. Haven't you ever been on a mud track during a rainstorm?"

"No, and I wish I wasn't now. I'm ready to get back to civilization."

He couldn't see it through the rain, but Spencer knew the ditch—as in, the monster ditch—was just ahead. Jethro wouldn't even try to fix it, maintaining that anyone he wanted to come to the ranch or leave it could do so with no problem. Which was just plain wrong. Anyone without a jacked-up pickup truck or, at the least, a four-wheel drive vehicle that rode high, would be stuck on one side or the other, if not the middle of the ditch. Spencer increased his speed, knowing the only way to get through the ditch was to get over and out of it before the wheels had a chance to dig into the mud.

Georgie was talking but he had no idea what she said. He was busy praying they made it through. He felt the thump shudder through the ambulance as they drove down into the ditch. "Yes!" he said as they came out the other side. But he celebrated too soon. They slid backward, back into the ditch.

The hind wheels stuck on something. Mud, a rock, who knew what. They boomeranged to a halt.

"Why are you stopping?"

"I'm not. Voluntarily, anyway." He started "rocking" the truck. He put it in reverse and slowly stepped on the gas. Then he did the same thing driving forward. He did that several times but it didn't help.

"What are you doing?"

"Rocking the truck. Haven't you ever been stuck in the mud?"

"No. I'm a city girl, remember?"

"Well, city girl, we're stuck," he said, resigned to getting out in the monsoon to see what he could do to get them loose.

"Stuck? We're stuck? Like, we can't get out?"

A little exasperated, he looked at her. "That's generally what stuck means, at least in this context."

He pulled out his cell phone and checked the bars. "No reception. That's no surprise."

"What do we do now?"

"Radio the station and see what's available. If that fails we'll have them try to find a wrecker." Although there was only one local wrecker and Spencer would bet his paycheck that guy was working overtime in this mess. He didn't think he'd tell Georgie that unless he had to.

"Try? What do you mean we'll have them try? We need to get back."

He keyed in the mic and explained the problem. After hearing a long explanation that basically said they were out of luck until much later, he ended the call, saying, "Okay, we'll figure something out. For that matter, I'm not positive the wrecker can find us. We're out at old man Caldwell's ranch. It's bad out here."

He turned to see Georgie gaping at him. "What is wrong with you? We'll figure something out? Are you insane?"

Spencer laughed. "Not last I looked." He paused and added, "Looking a little wild-eyed there, Georgie."

"Of course I'm wild-eyed. How in the hell do you expect to 'figure something out'? We're stuck in the mud in a ditch in a freaking monsoon with no help coming. What can you possibly do?"

He looked out the window. Yeah, it wasn't going to let up anytime soon. He sighed, put on the waterproof jacket that he'd taken off earlier, and grabbed the small hatchet everyone kept for an emergency. "Relax. I've done this before."

"Relax? You really are insane."

"I'm gonna need you to drive once I've gotten it prepared."

"How are you going to do that?"

"I'm going to wedge some stuff under the tires to see if we can get traction that way. Rocks, brush, tree limbs, a board would be nice but we don't have one."

He started to get out, but stopped when he realized she was getting dressed. "You don't need to get out in this."

"Of course I do. You need help. I'm the only other person here. I'm not playing the helpless female."

"Believe me, Georgie, that's the last thing I think of when I think of you."

Chapter Eight

*M*Y EDUCATION IS *sorely lacking.* Georgie had never been forced to get a truck—a heavy ambulance at that—out of the mud. She'd been on snow, in the mountains while on vacation, but with four-wheel drive, and no blizzard, of course it hadn't been a problem. Plus, it's not like she'd ever actually lived anywhere it snowed significantly. Central and South Texas didn't get a lot of the frozen white stuff, and neither did Fort Worth, where she grew up. As for the mud, she stuck to paved roads. If she'd wanted to go off-road she'd have bought an ATV.

She'd spoken the truth when she said she was a city girl. Until she came to Last Stand she'd only lived in cities. She hadn't been to the country much. And she sure as hell hadn't been out on a remote ranch in the middle of a flipping monsoon.

Grumbling to herself, she slogged around looking for branches. There were a couple of large oak trees nearby, so she and Spencer both checked there first. Although she was bundled up in her waterproof winter jacket, it was bitingly cold with the rain driving into her face. She found a large branch but couldn't move it more than a few inches by herself. She located Spencer easily enough, since like her, he wore his reflective gear. "I need some help."

He dropped off his load beside the ambulance and came to where she was beneath the big tree. He took one end and she took the other to carry/drag it over to the truck. "I'm going to split it so we can put it under both wheels," Spencer said, glancing around. "Good thing we got out from under that oak tree before—"

A flash of lightning lit up the sky, followed almost immediately by an ear-splitting crack and boom of thunder that seemed to go on forever. Georgie couldn't help flinching. *Oh, my God, that was close. Way too close.*

"Before that happened," Spencer finished. "Get in the truck. I'll take care of this."

"I can help."

"Get in the damn truck, Georgie," he said in a tone that brooked no argument.

But of course, she argued. "No. I'm helping you."

She couldn't really see his face but the way he had gritted out the words told her he was pissed. "Georgie, do you want to get struck by lightning?"

Another streak of lightning split the sky; another crack and boom of thunder rent the air. It sounded even closer. "No."

"Then get in the truck." He said it slowly, enunciating each word clearly.

"What about you?"

"If I get struck you can rescue me. I'll need CPR but I probably won't die."

"Probably? Are you kidding?"

"Actually, I was. Most likely neither of us will be struck by lightning. But just in case there's no point in both of us putting ourselves at risk."

Damn it, he was right. "Fine. But if you need help call me."

"I will. Now, please, get in the truck. I'll have this ready in a minute and you can drive the truck out. When you get out of the ditch keep going until you're well clear of it."

She got into the driver's seat and waited, probably about ten minutes but she couldn't get to her phone easily and with the ambulance turned off she couldn't see its clock either. Spencer rapped on the window. She started the truck and rolled it down.

"Do you know how to do this?"

It chapped her to admit it but it was too important to lie. "Not a clue."

"Start slow and give it gas gradually. I'll be pushing it, but I doubt that will matter much. Ready?"

"Be careful," she said.

"Count on it."

A little bit later she heard him beat on the back doors. She did exactly what he'd told her and by some miracle, she felt the truck moving forward. Keeping her foot on the gas and gradually increasing the speed, she felt a lurch and heard a shout from Spencer, and knew she was free. She kept going until she reached the top of the rise, made sure to park well away from the hill, and put on the emergency brake. She opened the door, jumped out and ran toward Spencer, who had reached the crest of the hill.

She could see his smile even through the gloom. He held up his hand for a high five and she smacked it. Then, somehow, they were in each other's arms and Spencer was twirling her around. "We did it!" she yelled, over sounds of the driving rain.

"We sure did."

They grinned at each other. And then their mouths met in a crushing kiss, with lips and tongues and teeth, and heat exploding in a torrent between them. It was stupid and ill advised and she didn't give one tiny damn. She only knew that she'd never felt such an adrenaline rush in her life. Spencer pulled back and looked at her, and instead of letting go, God help her, she pulled his head down and kissed him again.

The second kiss was as hot as the first. Hotter, even. She wanted to drink him in. Wanted to surrender to this need that flared and throbbed in her veins. Lips still together, he backed her toward the truck. She'd left the door open when she got out and he set her on the seat, stepping between her legs. His lips left hers and traveled to her neck, stringing kisses along the way. For a long moment, he stayed that way, with his lips setting her skin on fire.

He came back to her mouth and kissed her again. She answered, wrapping her arms around his neck and urging him closer. Spencer pulled back and looked into her eyes.

"Damn." He kissed her again, but briefly, sweetly. Leaning his forehead against hers, he said, "You have no idea how much I don't want to say this."

Somehow she got her heartbeat under control. "What—"

Yes, what in the hell are you doing? What were you thinking?

"We'd better get going."

A streak of lightning and a crack of thunder startled both of them. She jumped. Spencer loosened his hold on her but he still stood close.

"You need to move," she said. "If you want to drive."

"Huh? Oh." He moved and put out a hand to help her down.

Which she didn't need but she took it anyway. She slogged around the truck in the rain to the other side and got in.

Neither of them said a word. They took off their outerwear, Spencer cranked up the heat, put the truck in drive and drove onward.

※

BY THE TIME they hit the highway they still hadn't spoken. Spencer didn't know about Georgie, but he was even now, half an hour later, blown away.

But that was the adrenaline. Yeah, adrenaline. No wonder. Out in the middle of nowhere, stuck in a ditch, raining like shit with thunder and lightning. The kiss—the kisses were simply a reaction to a dangerous situation. That's all.

Bullshit. Those were the hottest kisses you've had in years. Maybe ever.

Oh, c'mon. Don't you think that's an exaggeration?

No. And neither do you. Admit it. That whole session was

smokin'.

He shot Georgie a glance. "Are you getting warm yet?" They'd both stripped off their outerwear and he had the heater blasting on full but it would be a while before he warmed up.

"Still cold but better." She spread her hands out in front of the warm air. "At least I don't feel like a Popsicle anymore." She was quiet for a bit, then said, "Spencer? Are we going to talk about it?"

"Talk about…"

"Yes. Are we going to talk about what happened back there? After we cleared the ditch."

He didn't want to. What could he say? He thought it had been fantastic. But that probably wasn't what she wanted to hear. But he knew one thing, and he said so. "I'm not apologizing."

"Why would you? That was as much my fault as yours."

"Why does it have to be anyone's *fault*?" He shot her another glance. He couldn't read her expression. "I'd do it again in a heartbeat. But not here. Not on duty."

"So would I."

He looked at her. "You would?"

She nodded. "Yes. If we weren't coworkers."

Well, shit. "But we are coworkers."

"Yes. So I don't think we should, um, do that again."

"You don't think we should kiss again."

"Right. It's better that way."

"Since we're coworkers."

"Right."

"And you don't date coworkers. Or kiss them either, apparently. Except that we did. Kiss, that is."

"You sound mad."

"I'm not mad. So we kissed. It's not a big deal."

"I know it's not. It only happened because of the situation."

That was going too far. "Bullshit. It happened because we're attracted to each other. And what's more, you know it."

"Whatever the reason, it won't happen again."

He could tell she was irritated by her frosty tone and the fact that her chin stuck out pugnaciously. Good, because he was annoyed as shit. "You sound awfully sure of that."

"I am."

"Fine. Your loss." He knew he was being a prick but he couldn't seem to help it.

"Wow. You must have an awfully strong back to be able to carry that ego around."

Where were all his famed comebacks? The only thing he could come up with was "Oh, yeah?" which was damned lame. So he said nothing.

By the time they pulled into the station he was beginning to see the humor of the situation. Not to mention, they needed to get along if they were going to work together. "Wait," he said before she could bolt out of the truck.

She turned and looked haughtily down her nose at him, which was funny in itself since her nose was a small, delicate thing. "What?" Her tone had gone from frosty to glacial.

"I'm sorry."

She lifted an eyebrow. "You said you weren't going to apologize."

"I'm not sorry for kissing you. I'm sorry I was a jerk about it afterward. Truce?" He held out his hand.

She shook his hand. "Truce." She smiled. "We'll just forget it, okay?"

"Sure." No way in hell was he forgetting it. Even if he wanted to he couldn't. He wondered if it would be that easy for her. Remembering her response, he didn't think so.

Chapter Nine

"WHEN DO THE toys get sorted?" Georgie asked Spencer the next day. They had met to collect toys from the bins they were responsible for, plus some others that people for one reason or another hadn't been able to get to. She suspected that was more common than not. Everyone had to know Spencer would do it if they couldn't—or, more likely, if they forgot.

"The Daughters of Last Stand try to sort them as they come in. But there's always a big rush at the end so that's why we cut it off early. The specific ones that people picked from the wishing tree at the library are supposed to be in one bag and tagged with the note from the tree. But then there are also general toys rather than the specific ones. The night of the twenty-third is busy with all the last-minute crap to take care of."

"That must be crazy."

"It is." He grinned at her. "But it's fun."

She and Spencer had very carefully avoided the topic of what had happened the night before. Georgie knew she was supposed to forget about it, and had had every intention of doing just that. But it wasn't working, damn it. Last night after she'd gone to bed, she'd even dreamed about the kiss. And more. It had been a very sexy dream and she had to work hard not to think about it every time she looked at Spencer. He didn't act as if it was at all hard for him to forget their kiss. Kisses.

"What are you doing after this?" Spencer asked her.

"Laundry. Why?"

"I have an idea. Have you been to Whiskey River?"

"The town just to the east of us? No, why?"

"It's an interesting little town. There's a metal artist over there who has some really interesting art. He's pretty well-known. His name is Gabe Walker."

"Oh, I've heard of him. I didn't realize he lived so close."

"We could go over to the Whiskey River art gallery, have some lunch over there, and maybe take in a movie. I'm even willing to go Christmas shopping if you want."

"That sounds like a date. Especially the offering to go Christmas shopping part."

"It's not." He grinned and added, "I have some Christmas shopping to do too."

She didn't answer, trying to figure out his ploy. Because it had to be a ploy. Didn't it?

"You can stay here and do laundry if you'd rather."

She gave in. "Christmas shopping or laundry. Gee, which one to choose? All right, I'll go. But it's not a date."

"Fine. You can buy me lunch."

"We'll go dutch."

"Whatever you say. Meet in the apartment parking lot in half an hour?"

"All right." Christmas shopping with Spencer. It was probably a mistake but she consoled herself, thinking she really did have some shopping to do and she wanted to see what Whiskey River was like.

※

WHISKEY RIVER WAS a charming little town that was only a fifteen-minute drive from Last Stand. Georgie hadn't been there yet, but she'd heard a lot about it. In fact, she'd looked at it online when she was job hunting, but Whiskey River's emergency services were county rather than from the town itself. She wanted to be more of a part of the community, and she was afraid she wouldn't be if she worked for the county, so she'd ended up in Last Stand, which had its own services.

"Do you go to Whiskey River often?" she asked Spencer.

"Depends. I go around Christmas because they have all sorts of things going on too. But today we're just looking for Christmas presents. And at the art gallery."

"Why don't we have an art gallery in Last Stand?"

"Because we don't have any artists?"

"I doubt that. Every town has an artist or two, don't they?"

"Yeah, but if we have artists they aren't professional. You can find stuff during festivals and Christmas markets and things like that. But nothing like what's in Whiskey River's art gallery. Wild Horse Gallery is its name. Do you want to go there first or look around on the square?"

"Let's go to the art gallery."

"There's also a really good bakery. So we can have a snack before dinner."

The gallery was even more impressive than it had sounded. There was a very large collection of works by Gabe Walker—everything from a huge dragon sitting outside in the back yard, to wall art, to tiny animals made out of metal. There were paintings by local artists, as well as paintings from well-known artists. There was a group of wood carvings of various animals that really caught Georgie's imagination.

"Look at this dog, Spencer. I swear I can see it wagging its tail and barking."

"It's good. Very lifelike. But look at this." He showed her a horse about a foot tall, carved out of a beautiful reddish-brown wood, rearing up on its hind legs. "My sister would kill to have this."

"It's beautiful. I bet it costs a fortune."

"Probably. But it can't hurt to ask."

A woman came over and asked if she could help.

"How much is this horse?" Spencer asked.

"Six hundred and fifty. It's a Robin Briarcliff."

The name meant nothing to Georgie but apparently Spencer was familiar with it.

"That's not a bad price for one of her pieces."

"It's one of her more affordable pieces," the woman agreed.

"I need to make a couple of calls," Spencer said as he pulled out his cell phone. A moment later he said, "Graham, it's me. Do you have a present for Jessie yet? Good. I've got something you and Turner can go in with me on. Turner probably doesn't have anything for her either but I'll call to make sure. Yeah, I'll get it and you can pay me back." He repeated the process with his other brother and the next thing she knew, he'd bought it and arranged for it to be giftwrapped and held for them until later that afternoon, before closing.

"Wow, when you make up your mind you don't mess around."

"When you see the perfect present you should jump on it. Besides, Jessie is hard to shop for. I mean, she's not into much besides horses. And a new saddle is way too expensive. Plus, this way Graham and Turner owe me big-time for finding something we can all go in on."

Georgie laughed. "You're mighty proud of yourself."

"Yep. Now, would you rather have a cookie from the bakery or look at the Kelly Boots store and then go for the cookies?"

"Cookies," she said promptly. "I haven't been able to think about anything else since you mentioned them."

Cookies & S'more(s)'s display window had a fully decorated gingerbread house, with a sign that invited people in to decorate another one inside. The sign said there was a new one each day. They walked in and were immediately assailed with the delicious aromas of gingerbread, cookies, and other delectable edibles.

"Hi, I'm Polly," the shop assistant said. "What can I help you with?"

"It all looks delicious." The display case had everything

from gingerbread cookies to Christmas s'mores. "There's no way I can decide," Georgie told Spencer.

"You can get more than one thing, you know."

"I know, but I shouldn't."

"It's Christmas—live a little."

"Talked me into it." Georgie chose several different cookies and a Christmas s'more. Polly packed them into a box.

"Are you planning to share?" Spencer asked.

"I could. But if you get your own we can try even more of them."

Spencer laughed and picked out another dozen. All different from the ones Jessie had chosen.

"Enjoy," Polly said, handing him his own box.

"If we eat all these cookies we'll be sick, or at the least, in a sugar coma."

"Yeah, but what a way to go."

"You have a point," she said and they both laughed.

On a table in the corner of the shop sat a partially decorated gingerbread house. "Remember when we decorated one at the Corbyns'?" Georgie asked. She glanced at Spencer. "This sign says we're welcome to decorate but they've obviously never seen what you can do with a gingerbread house."

"Hey, my side was inventive."

"Oh, that's what you call it?"

"Now you've hurt my feelings."

She shot him a glance. His voice held a teasing note but he did look a little upset. "I'm sorry. I was just kidding."

He laughed out loud. "You are so easy."

She punched him in the arm.

He rubbed his arm but said, "You hit like a girl."

"I am a girl. And I wasn't trying to hit you very hard."

The bell hanging over the door jangled and a man came in. He was tall, with dark blond hair and arresting blue eyes. He didn't have a coat on but wore a short-sleeved navy T-shirt over a broad chest that read, "We've Got Your Back" and in smaller print below that, "vetsandpets.org." And damn, was the man ripped.

"Spencer?" He walked over to them and put out his hand. "Good to see you, man. What are you doing in Whiskey River?"

"Eating cookies," Spencer said, shaking his hand. "Asher, this is my partner, Georgie Durant. Georgie, Asher Chapman."

"Firefighter or paramedic? Or both?" Asher asked, shaking her hand.

"Paramedic. I leave the firefighting to him. What is 'We've Got Your Back'?"

"It's a nonprofit that unites veterans and shelter animals."

"What a wonderful idea."

"Thanks. We can always use volunteers."

"Better watch it, Georgie. This guy could sell overcoats in Hell. And will if it will help We've Got Your Back. It's his brainchild."

Asher laughed. "Thanks for sending Clay to us, Spencer. He adopted a dog and is volunteering too."

"I'm glad you could help him."

"A little too soon to tell, but we're hopeful. Speaking of volunteers, I'd better pick up the cookies. They get cranky unless I feed them regularly."

"That really is a wonderful thing his organization is doing," Georgie said after they left the shop. "Is he a veteran?"

"Yes. Asher was Special Forces. A Green Beret. He lost a leg in Iraq and this nonprofit he started is his way of helping veterans."

"Really? He doesn't even have a limp."

"Artificial limbs have come a long way. And I think it's been over a year since he lost it."

"You've volunteered for them, haven't you?"

He shrugged. "A few times. Why?"

"Why aren't you married?"

"EXCUSE ME?" SPENCER said. Why wasn't he married? WTF? "What kind of question is that?"

"You're too good to be true. Everything you do is exemplary. Not only your profession but as if that wasn't enough, you volunteer to organize the toy drive. You volunteer to work with shelter animals and veterans. I know you help your sister on the ranch. I'm sure there are all sorts of things you volunteer for. In fact, you probably volunteer at every stinkin' charity organization Last Stand has, plus some in Whiskey River. My God, you even play dominoes once a week with a lonely old man. You're a—you're a damn paragon."

Paragon? Not hardly. "Fred's not lonely." He was no paragon. In fact, it made him feel weird that she might even believe it. He stuffed his hands in his pockets. "Lots of people volunteer. It's not a big deal." He liked volunteering. He liked helping people, and working on different projects helped keep him from being bored.

"Yes, it is. You must have some deep, dark secret. Otherwise why aren't you married or at least involved with someone?"

That was easy enough to answer. "Because I haven't found the woman I want to be with the rest of my life."

"Have you even had a serious relationship?"

No. Not really. Some lasted longer than others but even those hadn't been serious. "What does that have to do with anything?"

"You haven't."

So? He hadn't even hit thirty yet. What was the rush? "How many have you had, smart-ass?"

"Just one. But he was like you. He couldn't or wouldn't make a commitment. Never mind me, though. We were talking about you."

"Why do you want to know?"

She looked at him like he'd smacked her in the face. "I—I—Oh, never mind."

He backed her up against the wooden slats of the building they'd been walking by. "Could it be because you're interested in me yourself?"

"No, I told you I don't date—"

"Coworkers. Yes, I know. Maybe I haven't gotten really involved with anyone because I was waiting for you."

Her eyes were huge. "M-m-me?"

"Oh, hell," he said and kissed her.

Her lips were soft and inviting. Her tongue touched his, tentatively at first, but then she tangled hers with his and his blood fired like a three-alarm blaze. He wanted more. Wanted to cup her bare breasts in his hands, slide his hands and lips all over her naked body, boost her up against the wall and—

Oh, Jesus, what was he thinking? He lifted his mouth and gazed into her eyes. He read shock and desire in their blue depths. But not anger. And not, unbelievably, regret.

If they hadn't been in public God knows what would have happened.

He opened his mouth to apologize but she cut him off. By tugging his head down and kissing him. She thrust her tongue inside his mouth and he met her stroke for stroke. He was hard and aching for her and he knew there was absolutely nothing he could do about that now. But he wanted to. Damn, he wanted to.

She pulled back. "Um, wow. That kinda got out of hand."

Reluctantly, he let go of her, but he stayed where he was. "Kinda?"

"We should go," she said, ignoring his comment. "I want to look at the Kelly Boots shop."

"Not yet."

"Why not?"

He simply looked at her.

"Oh."

"Yes. Oh."

She bit her lip and he could see she was struggling not to laugh. She lost that battle and let out a peal of laughter.

"I'm glad you're enjoying this."

It took her a minute to get control of herself. "Oh, lighten up. I have to say, we pick the most inappropriate times to—"

"Make out?"

"I was going to say kiss. But I guess it was a little more than that."

"Ya think?"

"I think we should talk about this later. For now, I'm going into Kelly Boots. Are you going with me?"

"Lead on."

Half an hour later, Georgie walked out of Kelly Boots with a brand-new pair of cowboy boots. Pink and white and sparkly. Even though she had red hair, she said she wore pink sometimes and she'd fallen in love with the boots.

Women are weird. To Spencer, cowboy boots were for working on the ranch so most of his boots were functional rather than fancy. He did have a really nice pair of black boots for more formal occasions. But women... His sister had God knows how many pairs of boots. Obviously, she wore them for working on the ranch, but she had other fancy-ass boots with colors and sparkles and beads and whatnot. That girl loved her some cowboy boots and apparently, so did Georgie.

They walked around the square, decorated for Christmas with lights and garlands. The shops were ready for Christmas as well, with appropriate window dressings. There was a huge decorated tree in the middle of the square itself. They went inside several of the shops that interested them. Whiskey River was a pretty town. People from Last Stand visited Whiskey River often and vice versa.

"Fallen Angels? What's that?" Georgie asked, stopping at a window with a wooden sign proclaiming the name.

"Judging from what's in the window, it's lingerie. And no, I do not want to go in there with you. I'll wait for you on that bench over there," he said, motioning to a bench a few doors down.

"Chicken."

"Yes, ma'am." He added a clucking sound.

Georgie rolled her eyes and went inside the shop.

Right. Go into a shop with all kinds of sexy, silky girly stuff with Georgie? Not happening. He wasn't a masochist.

※

GEORGIE COULDN'T REMEMBER when she'd had so much fun. In Last Stand she'd been too busy either working or handing out flyers and checking barrels to have much time to simply enjoy the shops. She was going to fix that once she got back. But in the meantime, she had fun buying things for her family as well as for herself. She missed them, especially during the holidays, but she had plans to go see them on Christmas Day. She wondered if her sister would have had the baby by then, but she still had a few weeks to go until her due date.

She wished she'd had a picture of Spencer's face when he realized she wanted to go into Fallen Angels. The proprietors, Chantel and Angel Chandler, had been great, finding some lingerie that was perfect for her, as well as a wrap that she couldn't resist. And they about died laughing when she told them about Spencer's horrified expression. "We get that a lot," Chantel said. "But once they come in they're usually fine."

Spencer said he knew a great place to eat near Whiskey River. He took her to a restaurant called Blue, out next to the Barrels winery, which was a little north of town. She'd been afraid she wasn't dressed appropriately but Spencer said it was casual. The restaurant was very pretty. It was new, fresh and a bit modern. The hostess led them to a small table along the side of the room, one of the half-circle booths with beige cushions. It was next to a window from which you could see the grape vines, which naturally this time of year were bare. But she bet it was beautiful in the spring and summer.

The tables were wood topped and the wooden rafters of the high ceilings were made from the same wood, though they had a rough finish rather than the smooth finish of the tables. Artwork adorned the walls. Spencer said it was all from local artists and for sale. The art was a mix of both modern and traditional, and surprisingly went well together. The lighting was subdued but not too dark. In the background soft jazz and rhythm and blues played.

They ordered drinks—beer for both of them—and told the server to come back for their food order.

"This is very romantic," Georgie said, looking around. "Did you pick it for that reason?"

"No, I picked it because it has really good food. The romantic atmosphere is just a bonus."

She shook her head. "The last thing we need is a romantic atmosphere. I'm not sure what to do. About us."

"You mean the fact that given half a chance we can't keep our hands off each other?"

She frowned at him, though she had to admit he was right. "Yes. Because I still haven't changed my mind about dating a coworker."

"Because of what happened with your ex?"

"More like what didn't happen," she said tartly. "Besides, what if we start dating and then break up and still have to work together?"

He shrugged. "So we get new partners. It's not as if we don't both work with other people. Besides, I don't believe we'd ever hate each other so much that we couldn't even work together occasionally."

That wasn't always the problem. She didn't hate Cole. But seeing him constantly and working with him once they'd broken up had been hell. That was one of the main reasons she moved, after all.

Should she admit she was tempted? Hell, he probably already knew that. She looked at him. He was smiling in that way that set her heart to fluttering. Oh, yeah, he knew. Damn, did the man have to be so appealing? She'd come to town intending to take a break from men. It shouldn't have been that difficult. But Spencer was tempting her to forget all about that resolve.

"See anything on the menu that looks good?" Spencer asked.

"This brisket Benedict looks interesting, but I don't think I could eat the whole thing."

"Thin sliced beef brisket, with poached eggs, hollandaise, and a drizzle of barbecue sauce on a cheddar jalapeno corn bread waffle," Spencer read. "I bet it's really good. I don't think I've had anything here yet that wasn't good."

"I'd say we could split it but I'm sure that wouldn't be enough for you."

"It would if we ordered several small plates. Why don't they just call them appetizers?"

"Because they're not. They're teeny tiny tastes of things."

Spencer looked at the menu again. "Maybe we should get one of everything."

She laughed. "They probably have a combo. Let's try that."

Over dinner they talked about their respective families. Georgie actually knew a lot about the McBrides. She'd met both of Spencer's brothers at the hospital through work and had gotten to know Jessie better at the get-together that Audrey had arranged the week before.

"So tell me about your family," Spencer said. "I know your sister is due to have a baby. Has she had it yet?"

"No. Technically she's not due until New Year's Eve, but like I told you, she's pretty anxious."

"Do you like her husband?"

"Paul? Yes, he's great. And loves my sister madly."

"So you're a romantic."

"About some things," she admitted. "It's nice to see a relationship that's working."

"Your family lives in Fort Worth?"

"Yes. I was born and raised there."

"How did you end up in Houston?"

"After I got my certification I went job hunting. I wound up in Houston." And almost immediately fell for Cole.

Spencer ate a bite of the brisket. Then he looked at her like he was trying to decide whether to say something or not. He shrugged. "That's where you met your ex."

"Yes. I can't believe it took me so long to figure out that was never going to work."

"You realize you're still letting him call the shots, don't you?"

"What?" She stared at him. "I sure as hell am not. Why would you say that?"

"Think about it. Your refusal to go out with a coworker means he still has power over you. You're letting one bad relationship dictate who you do or don't date."

She started to deny it again but he had a point. She didn't like it, but she could see it might seem that way. "It wasn't all bad. He's not a bad person. He's just commitment phobic."

"You broke up. Your decision. Which means it wasn't good."

God, he was annoying when he was right. "Do we have

to talk about my ex? Why can't we talk about some of your exes?"

"Because I don't have any, remember?"

"You really haven't dated anyone for longer than a few dates?"

"No, I have. But it was never a long-term thing. Their choice as much as mine," he added.

She doubted that but there was no point in arguing. He clearly believed it.

Once they finished eating Georgie said, "I'm really glad I'm not driving home."

"Why? You only had one beer."

"I think I'm going into a food coma."

He laughed. "So, no dessert?"

"I'll eat my leftover cookies. Tomorrow. In the meantime, here." She handed him her credit card. "Just ask the waiter to split the check down the middle. I'll be back."

She thought he might argue but he simply shook his head and muttered something under his breath. "What's that?" she asked.

"I don't like taking your money." He looked up at her and grinned. "My mama didn't raise me that way."

"From what I've heard about your mother, she's very much an independent, modern woman."

"Oh, she is. But she raised her boys to be Southern gentlemen. And Southern gentlemen don't take a woman's money."

"Sorry. You'll just have to deal with it." Dang, he was so cute when he grinned like that.

Chapter Ten

S PENCER WAS SUPPOSED to meet Turner at the Saloon for a beer and a game of pool. He ordered a beer and while Slater went off to get it, Turner called and canceled on him. Something about Charlie wanting him to go Christmas shopping with her. He shrugged it off, but since Graham had gotten married and Turner and Charlie had gotten together, it seemed like his brothers canceled on him more often than not. But it didn't bother him. Much.

Maybe he was just jealous that they'd both found a woman to fall madly in love with.

Whoa. A woman to fall madly in love with? When did you decide you wanted to settle down?

I didn't say right this minute. But someday I'd like to.

Yeah, the idea of being with a woman for longer than a few dates was a lot more appealing than it used to be. But he didn't have anyone special in mind.

What a crock of shit. He'd been thinking about Georgie since he met her. Thinking that she might even be the one. But first he had to convince her to date him. How would either of them know if they could work if she would only go out with him at random times that she refused to call a date?

Slater set his beer down in front of him and stopped to talk for a moment.

"When are you getting the new pool table?" Spencer asked. Slater had been planning on buying a new one for months now.

"Changed my mind," Slater said, smiling.

"Too expensive?"

"Nope. I just decided I like this one."

There's a story there, Spencer thought, but he had no idea what it was.

"So where's Turner?" Slater asked. "Didn't you say you were meeting him here?"

"Yeah, but he crapped out on me. And here I was, ready to kick his ass at the pool table."

"I'll play a game with you," said a man sitting a few barstools down from him. "But don't get your heart set on kicking my ass. I'm afraid you're the one who's going to get his ass kicked."

No way could Spencer resist a challenge like that. "You're on," he said, and held out his hand. "Spencer McBride."

"Cole Baxter," the other man said as they shook. He was a big dude, a little taller and a little broader than Spencer. The kind of guy you'd rather have on your side than against you.

They settled on five bucks a game. Not enough to hurt either if they lost, but hey, it was money. And, more importantly, competition. They played for a while, talking about sports mostly. Spencer won the first game. Barely.

Cole won the next one. Barely.

"Best two out of three?" Spencer asked. "But I need a beer first."

"I could go for another beer. And best two out of three. But let's make it more interesting. Double or nothing?"

"Took the words out of my mouth. Sure." They both went to the bar and ordered a couple of beers. While they waited, Spencer said, "Are you new in town or just visiting? I haven't seen you around."

"Just visiting."

"Will you be sticking around a while?"

"I don't know. Depends on how things go." He drank some of his beer and added, "Depends on a woman, actually."

"I've been there," Spencer said sympathetically, thinking of Georgie.

"Who hasn't?" Cole asked.

They started another game. It was close but just as Cole was about to sink the eight ball to win he happened to glance toward the door and he missed his shot by a mile.

Spencer looked to see what had blown the guy's concentration. Georgie and Audrey had just walked in and were standing framed in the doorway. And Cole had straightened and was staring at the two.

No. He couldn't be...

"Cole? Do you want a do-over?"

Cole laughed and seemed to collect himself. "Yeah, but not for the game." He pulled out his wallet and tossed his money down. "The woman I came here to see just walked in."

Shit. Damn. Hell. "Which one?" he asked without much hope.

"The redhead."

"Which one?" Spencer repeated. "They're both redheads."

"The one on the left," Cole said as he started toward the door.

Shit. He should have known. Georgie.

Cole was her ex? Cole, the nice guy he'd been playing pool with? The guy who, apparently, wanted her back?

Great. He was screwed.

※

"WHO IS THAT hunk coming toward us?" Audrey asked. "Do you know him? 'Cause I sure don't."

"What hunk?" Georgie asked, looking in the direction Audrey indicated. "Oh…shit."

"So you do know him. Who is he? Good God, he's absolutely gorgeous."

What in the hell was Cole doing here? "That," she said with resignation, "is Cole Baxter. Aka my ex-boyfriend."

"Oh, my God, Georgie. That's your ex?"

"Yes. Would you like to meet him?"

"Sure, but he's obviously not interested in anyone but you."

Georgie stood rooted to the spot. She was shocked to see him. But not, thank God, all that happy about it. Her heart wasn't thumping madly like it used to do whenever she saw him. She wasn't unhappy because he'd made it clear— again—that he wasn't interested in settling down. No, she was simply surprised.

"Georgie," he said as he reached them. "It's so good to see you." He put his arms around her to hug her and would have kissed her on the mouth, but she foiled his attempt by turning her head so he only got her cheek.

"What are you doing here, Cole?" She managed to step away. Audrey elbowed her. "Cole, this is my friend, Audrey Stockton. Audrey, this is Cole Baxter."

He looked at Audrey and gave her his trademark smile. Which Georgie admitted was extremely effective. "Nice to meet you, Audrey."

"You too," Audrey said. She appeared a bit stunned.

Georgie didn't blame her. Cole was great to look at. And a nice guy. She'd never denied that. Dark hair, beautiful blue eyes, and the killer body beneath the long-sleeved black T-shirt and blue jeans he wore were enough to stun any woman. Thank God he didn't affect her like that anymore.

Really?

Damn straight.

"Oh, look, there's someone I need to talk to," Audrey said brightly and left them.

"We might as well sit down and you can tell me what you're doing here."

"Sure. But let me get you a drink first. Beer?"

"Fine." He knew what she liked. Or he should.

Audrey was talking to Spencer at the bar. Spencer waved

at her and she waved back. He pointed at Cole and raised his eyebrows, mouthing, "That's him?"

She shrugged and rolled her eyes. *Why the hell is Cole here?*

Cole returned with her beer and one for himself. "I've missed you, Georgie. I didn't realize how much until you left town."

Georgie realized with a start that since she'd come to Last Stand she really hadn't missed Cole. She hadn't thought about him often either. Maybe she really was over him.

The man she had been thinking of more and more often was over at the bar talking to Audrey.

"Georgie?"

"Oh, sorry. I was thinking about something else."

He looked a little taken aback. He wasn't accustomed to her not hanging on his every word. Okay, that was an exaggeration, but for her not to pay any attention to him was a definite first. He recovered quickly, though. "How's the new job? Do you like it?"

"Yes, I like it a lot."

"So…you like living in a small town? You never have before."

"I've never actually lived in one before. I didn't know whether I'd like it or not. But I do. I love it here. Last Stand is a great place to live. I always liked the Texas Hill Country whenever I visited." She drank some beer.

"I can't imagine living anywhere but the city. I never envisioned you as a small-town girl, either."

"People change."

"Yes, they do. And speaking of that—"

"Don't, Cole."

"Don't what? I haven't said anything."

"You haven't said why you're here."

"To see you. Obviously."

"Now you've seen me. I'm sorry but I came here with a friend and I don't want her to think I blew her off." She got up.

He caught her hand. "You're bound to know why I'm here."

"I can guess." Cole was going to tell her he'd changed his mind. And she didn't know how she felt about that. Once she'd have jumped at the chance. But now...she'd changed. She wasn't the same woman who was willing to wait forever while a man made up his mind about how serious he was about her. "And I don't want to hear it."

She tugged her hand away and left him to go to the bar. Audrey was still talking to Spencer when she cornered them. "You have to help me," Georgie said, grabbing Spencer's arm.

"Help you do what?"

"Did you see that man I was talking to?"

Spencer glanced at the table she'd just left. "Yeah. Your ex. Cole Baxter."

"How did you know? Audrey, did you tell him?"

"Not me," Audrey said. "What's the deal, Georgie? Why are you hiding from him?"

"I'm not hiding. Exactly. I'm trying to avoid any deep discussions."

"Why?" Spencer asked. "He seems like a nice guy."

"He is. But how do you know that?"

Spencer shrugged. "We played a few games of pool."

Pool? Spencer and Cole had played pool together? WTH? "Audrey, would you mind going and talking to Cole? I won't be long."

"Me? What am I supposed to say to the man? I met him for ten seconds."

"I don't care. Just chatter at him. Please?" She turned her best pleading expression on her friend.

Audrey sighed. "Okay, but you owe me."

After she left Georgie looked at Spencer. She realized she was still clinging to his arm. But she didn't release him. "I have a favor to ask you."

He looked at her hand, then back up to her face. "And what would that favor be?"

"Would you pretend to be my boyfriend?"

꒰ꕤ꒱

"YOU WANT ME to what?" Spencer stared at Georgie, wondering if he'd heard her correctly.

"I want you to be my boyfriend. Just for a couple of days."

Yeah, he'd heard that right. "Why?"

"Why do you think? I'm trying to discourage Cole before he tries to convince me that he wants to get back together."

Damn. "Are you sure that's what he wants?" Of course, Spencer knew it was. When he'd asked if Cole wanted a do-over, he'd said, "*Yeah. But not for the game.*"

"He hasn't said it yet, but I think that's where he's headed."

"Why don't you just be honest with him?"

"Because I'm not sure what I want. Duh."

"If you're not sure then you should let him have his say." Which about killed him to say, but if she really cared about the guy then she should have him.

Dumbass. Take her up on it!

No. I'm not that desperate.

You're not?

"You don't understand."

Spencer propped one foot on the footrest at the bottom of the barstool. "Explain it to me. I'm sure I'll get it. I'm very bright."

"Cole is very persuasive. I'm afraid if I talk to him and he wants to get back together I'll cave and say yes. And I'm not sure that's what I want."

"But you're not sure you *don't* want to get back together with him either. Are you?"

"We broke up months ago. If he'd really wanted to be with me again, then why did he wait so long? I just moved here. I like my job. I like Last Stand. I like—" She broke off, then said, "I like the people here."

God, you really are a dumbass, McBride. Grasping at straws. He seriously doubted she'd been about to say, "I like you." Damn it.

Besides, he knew she liked him. But that didn't mean she was through with Cole. "I don't understand why you can't just tell him, rather than run this scam on him."

"It's not a scam. Exactly."

Seemed like one to him. He shrugged. "If you're sure you want me to pretend to be your boyfriend, I'll do it on one condition."

"Anything. Scratch that. Almost anything."

"Go to the Christmas Ball with me. As my date."

She stared at him. "If I go to the Christmas Ball with you, as your date, you'll pretend to be my boyfriend?"

"I will. Even though I think you should be honest with him."

"Thank you!" She threw her arms around him and hugged the stuffing out of him. Releasing him, she said, "Come on." She grabbed his hand and pulled him along with her. "He won't dare bring up anything now."

He was probably going to regret this but what the hell.

"Spencer said you two had already met," she said when they reached the table.

Spencer noticed Audrey looked both relieved and annoyed. "You owe me," she mouthed to Georgie. He had to hide a grin. Georgie was racking up the IOUs.

Cole stood and nodded at him. "We played a little pool earlier."

"So he told me. Spencer is my partner. He's a firefighter paramedic."

"Oh? We didn't get that far."

"He's also my boyfriend." She gave Spencer a hard stare. He put his arm around her casually.

Cole stared at her and then turned his gaze to Spencer.

"We definitely didn't get that far. Why didn't you say something?" he asked Spencer.

"Why would I? I didn't know who you were until Georgie and Audrey walked in. I figured it out then."

He shrugged. "Fair point. Moving a little fast, aren't you, Georgie?"

"Only when compared to slower than molasses," Georgie snapped.

Audrey got up and said, "Don't mind me. I'm going to get a drink."

"You don't have to leave," Georgie said.

"Oh, yes," Audrey said. "I do."

"It was nice to meet you, Audrey," Cole said.

Audrey gave him a fleeting smile and left.

Damn, he's polite too. Why couldn't he be a troll or a jerk? Because your luck isn't that good.

"Can I talk to you a minute?" Cole asked Georgie. "Alone?"

"Uh…"

Spencer felt her hesitation but there was only so much he was willing to do. "I'll go get us all a beer."

"Not for me. Thanks," Cole said. "I'm driving. Staying at the Bluebonnet Inn."

And of course he doesn't drink too much and drive. The guy's a flipping paragon. Spencer patted Georgie on the ass and left, grinning at the dirty look she gave him.

Chapter Eleven

DAMN SPENCER. WHY did he have to leave? She sighed and looked at Cole. She remembered how she'd felt when they first broke up, months ago. Awful. She really didn't want to go through that again. And while she could admit that Cole was not a bad person, she didn't think she could ever trust him.

"All right, we're alone. What did you want to say to me?"

"Can I see you tomorrow? Somewhere a little more private?"

"I don't think that's a good idea."

"Afraid to be alone with me?"

"No. But I don't think we have anything to talk about." Then she uttered the clincher. "Besides, I'm working tomorrow."

"With McBride."

She nodded. "He's my partner."

"And your boyfriend."

"Right."

"I'm not sure I believe you. You just met him, didn't you?"

"Some things are instantaneous." She sighed and tried to

look blissful. "We met under the mistletoe at a party." Which was true. "I'd only been here a week or so and he'd been out of town until that night." Also true. "When we kissed, we both just knew."

"You kissed a man you didn't even know under the mistletoe? That doesn't sound like you."

It wasn't like her, and he knew it and had called her on it. Before she could think of an answer Spencer returned and set down a beer in front of her. "Spencer, Cole doesn't believe we met under the mistletoe and that I kissed you."

"He's right. You didn't."

She stared at him. "What—"

"Not the first time. But about the fifth or sixth time we decided it was fate. That's when she kissed me. Or I kissed her. I'm not sure which."

"And we've been together ever since," Georgie said.

"Sounds like quite a story," Cole said, with a bit of a sarcastic drawl. "I take it your department has no problem with you two being partners?"

"Neither did ours," Georgie pointed out. "When we worked together in Houston."

"We weren't partners," he reminded her.

"True. We'd probably have broken up long before we did if we had been."

"I'm going to head back to my hotel. Since you're working tomorrow can I see you Saturday?"

"Spencer and I are going to the Christmas Ball."

"All day?"

"No, of course not. But—" She cast around for something to say when Spencer took over the conversation.

"You might as well meet with him, Georgie. Let him have his say."

"Georgie doesn't need your permission to see me."

"I didn't say she did," Spencer said.

"I'll meet you on Saturday," Georgie told Cole before the two men got into it. "Eleven o'clock at the pie shop on Main. Char-Pie. Audrey is one of the owners."

"That's not exactly private."

"Take it or leave it."

"I'll take it." He got up. "I'll see you Saturday, Georgie." He turned to Spencer and said, "I'd say it was nice to meet you but I don't think it was."

Spencer just laughed.

Once Cole left Georgie turned to Spencer. "What was that about? Let him have his say? You were supposed to be helping me avoid him."

Spencer set down his beer. "Don't you think you were a little hard on him?"

Astonished, she stared at him. "Are you kidding? No."

"He obviously wants you back. And you won't even give him a chance, much less listen to him."

"You—I—This is none of your business."

"Excuse me, but as your fake boyfriend it sure as hell is."

Oh, yeah, she'd forgotten that. He had a point. Not that she'd admit it to him. "I have a very good reason for not wanting to see him."

"What is it?"

She gritted her teeth. "I don't want to talk about it."

"That's what I thought."

"What does that mean?"

"It means you're obviously not over the guy."

"You're so irritating. And you're so wrong."

Wasn't he?

***

SO GEORGIE WAS hung up on her ex. That explained why she kept refusing to date him. He and Georgie definitely had some chemistry going on. He didn't think that was fake. But she wasn't over Cole. And Spencer McBride didn't play second fiddle to anyone. No matter how much he wanted a woman.

Keep telling yourself that, buddy.

Sometimes his subconscious was irritating as shit.

Today Spencer was working the fire department while Georgie was on for EMS. So he wasn't sure how much he'd see her. But if he could grab a minute with her he was going to cut her loose from their date. Better that than being somewhere with a woman who wanted to be with someone else.

He got his chance a couple of hours into the shift. "I need to talk to you," he told Georgie.

"Okay. What about?"

"You don't have to go to the Christmas Ball with me."

"You're breaking the date? Why?"

"Look, Georgie, it's okay. You're going to see Cole tomorrow and you two are going to get back together."

"No, we're not. I told you that."

"Why? You still care about him. Don't deny it."

"Yes, I care about him. But that doesn't mean I'm still in love with him."

"Doesn't it?"

"Come with me." She led him to the room with the toys they'd collected. Which was a mistake because it made him think about the huge amount of toys yet to be tagged and wrapped.

"Damn, we need to get busy here."

"Never mind that. Sit down." He did so but she stayed standing. "I dated Cole for two years. We were colleagues for another year before that. We never had a discussion about the two of us that didn't end with him saying he was 'not ready' to commit," she said, making air quotes.

"So, he went out with other women while you were together?"

"No. At least, not as far as I knew. We were exclusive but he couldn't take the next step."

"The next step being marriage."

"The next step being living together. Or some kind of indication that he was planning on settling down with me someday. I finally got tired of waiting for him to make up his mind and broke up with him. And he let me. We weren't together for several months before I moved. So it's not like he didn't have the chance to do something before I moved away. He had plenty of chances."

"If you're so over him why am I pretending to be your boyfriend?"

Their tones sounded at the same time. Minutes later a fire engine and ambulance headed out. When they arrived, there were flames coming from the back end of the house but a neighbor had managed to get the elderly lady who lived there out.

"My dog and cat are in there. Please, can't someone get them out?"

"Where are they?" Spencer asked.

"I don't know. Maybe in the kitchen. Buffy got me out of there but when I turned around she was gone."

"Buffy is—"

"My dog. I think she went back for Vamp."

Vamp? "Your cat?"

"Yes, please save them. They're all I have."

"Let me check you out, ma'am," Georgie said to the woman. "The firefighters will do their best to save your pets."

Spencer left them and saw Cable, manning one of the hoses. "Dog and a cat. I'm going in."

Fortunately, they had arrived early enough to halt the fire before the home became fully involved. Spencer found the dog—a large German shepherd—in the kitchen, lying on its side with the cat next to it, meowing pitifully. He put the dog over his shoulder and the cat in his backpack and headed out.

Once outside he laid the dog down on the grass and Cable took the cat. Since the dog—Buffy—wasn't responsive, he performed CPR until someone handed him a pet oxygen mask. Shortly after he put that on the dog, she began breathing on her own.

By then the elderly lady was standing beside him holding her cat. He'd glimpsed Cable giving the cat oxygen while he was working on the dog. When the lady saw Buffy moving, she burst into tears. "I don't know how to thank you. You and that other nice fireman. And you, of course, young lady," she said to Georgie.

Georgie laughed. "Luckily I didn't have to do much for you, ma'am. These guys—" she motioned to the fire crew "—deserve the thanks."

The fire took about half an hour to extinguish. He saw Georgie later, back at the station when he was headed for the shower.

"You earned your hero badge today," she said.

"Nah. I'm just glad the animals made it. But Buffy and Vamp? Does that come from—"

"*Buffy the Vampire Slayer*. Yes, she says she still watches reruns and it was one of her favorite shows. Mostly because the heroine is kick-ass. Which I had to agree with. I like kick-ass heroines too."

"Somehow, Georgie, this doesn't surprise me at all."

GEORGIE FIGURED THAT Cole would already be at Char-Pie waiting for her when she arrived. He was always on time, unless he got called out on a job. She tried but somehow she usually just barely made it in time or was a few minutes late. She remembered it used to drive him crazy that she wasn't ready to go a half hour early. Only one of the things that had annoyed him about her, but he'd clearly forgotten that in her absence.

She waved at Charlie, Audrey's sister, but didn't get any pie. Cole sat at one of the small tables toward the back, with his empty plate in front of him. He got up as she walked toward him and pulled out her chair for her. Polite, as always.

"I'm glad you showed up. I wasn't sure you would," Cole said.

"I said I would. What did you want to see me about? I've got a lot to do so let's skip the small talk."

He looked a little surprised but said, "I've missed you."

"So you said. Apparently you didn't miss me before now. What changed?"

He rubbed the back of his neck. "You left town. Since then I've been thinking about us all the time. I was used to seeing you at work and then suddenly, you weren't there." He reached for her hand. She let it lie unresponsive in his. "I screwed up."

"In what way?" She admitted she was curious as to what he planned to say.

"I should never have let you break up with me."

"That wasn't your choice. You didn't 'let' me. I chose to break up with you."

"Because I wouldn't make a commitment. But, Georgie, even before you left I was questioning if I was doing the right thing. From the moment we broke up I questioned why I didn't try to stop you."

"You sure as hell didn't seem worried about it at the time."

"I wasn't. For about five minutes. But I've missed you. I've missed us. I didn't realize how much you meant to me until you were really gone. Until I couldn't see you nearly every day."

She pulled her hand away. "Cole, I don't want to be mean—"

"Just listen. Don't say anything yet. I know I hurt you. I'd give anything if I could go back and fix this. But I can't. All I can do is tell you I'm sorry and ask you to give me another chance."

She crossed her arms over her chest and looked at him. "If you'd asked me before I moved, I might have said yes. It would have been a mistake, but I probably would have. But as it is, I've moved on."

"With McBride." She lifted a shoulder in agreement. "Are you really involved with him?"

"I told you he was my boyfriend."

"I know what you told me. I'm asking you whether it's true."

Her mind was made up. There was no reason not to tell him the truth. "No. Not yet."

"What does that mean?"

"It means we're headed that way."

"But you're not involved. Yet, anyway."

She shook her head. "Not exactly," she said, thinking about those kisses.

"Why did you pretend you were?"

"I thought it would be easier. I thought we could avoid this," she said, motioning between the two of them. "I didn't want to get into a long discussion about what went wrong. So I figured if you thought I was with someone else you wouldn't push me."

"If you're not with McBride that means there's still a chance for you and me."

"No, it doesn't. I'm sorry but there's not a chance. Not any longer."

"So now you're going to wait for McBride?"

"No, I'm going to see what happens. I've been turning him down because I was afraid of going through the same thing I went through with you. I realized I wasn't giving him a chance. I automatically assumed he'd hurt me too. But I don't think he will. And if he does, I'll deal with it."

"What if it doesn't work out?"

"It won't make any difference between you and me. I'm done, Cole. I can't go back."

"So that's it. After everything we shared you're just done."

"I waited for you for months. I kept telling myself that I understood. You weren't ready. You loved me but I had to be patient. But you never changed. You were never *going* to change. You never made me feel like I was important to you. And I was fed up with being patient. That's why I moved. Why I got a new job."

"I'm telling you now. I love you. I want you back. Will you give me a chance?"

"It's too late." The words to the old Carole King song

that her mom used to play all the time came back to her: *Something inside has died.* And she realized that was true. She didn't feel the same. She didn't feel torn. She still cared about Cole, and probably always would. But she no longer wanted a future with him.

"Take some time to think about it," he said. "You don't have to give me an answer now."

"I don't want to hurt you, Cole, but I also don't want to string you along. We're over. We both need to move on."

"There's nothing I can do to change your mind? What if I moved here?"

Her jaw dropped open. Those were words she'd never thought to hear from Cole. "You love Houston. You don't want to leave there."

"I don't want to lose you. If that's what it takes for us to be together, I'm willing."

"If I was crazy enough to take you up on it, you'd resent me before you even got here. Face it, Cole. There's no fixing us."

He didn't say anything for a long moment. Then he sighed and said, "I guess there's no reason for me to hang around."

"I'm sorry."

"So am I. But it's my fault for not figuring out what—who—I wanted sooner."

"I'll walk out with you." Georgie felt badly for him but she also felt a sense of relief.

"Where's your car?" he asked when they got outside.

"I walked. My apartment is only a few blocks away."

He kissed her on the cheek and said, "If you change your mind, call me."

I won't, she thought but didn't say it. No reason to rub it in.

Chapter Twelve

A FTER HER CONVERSATION with Cole, Georgie thought she would have at least been a little sad that they were truly over. But she wasn't. She wasn't mad at him and she was sorry to hurt him. She still thought he was a nice person, but she was definitely no longer in love with him.

Because, she admitted, she'd fallen for Spencer. Sometime during the last month she'd fallen for him. If she wasn't in love, she was close to it. But how could she be in love when she'd spent the whole time she'd known him denying she wanted to be with him?

Well, she was done with that. No more hiding behind her coworker ban. Just because she worked with Spencer didn't mean that their relationship was doomed from the first. Besides, it wasn't as if she'd been dating Spencer for years, like she had Cole. Who knew what might happen between them? If she let it.

She remembered running into Spencer just before they came off shift early that morning. Spencer had asked her again if she was sure about going to the ball with him.

"I don't want to break the date," she'd said. "Do you?"

"No, but I also don't want to feel like I'm making you go

with me if you'd rather be with Cole."

"I told you, Cole and I are through. I'm seeing him a little later today and making sure he knows it."

He had studied her for a minute. "All right. But let me know if you change your mind."

"I won't. What time are you picking me up?"

"Around eight. See you later."

He hadn't added maybe, but he might as well have.

Later that evening Georgie opened her door to Spencer and did a double take. She was accustomed to seeing him at work, or at most wearing a nice pair of jeans. Spencer didn't have to try hard to look good but Spencer McBride in a tux was a heart-stopping sight.

They both stood there staring at each other and then Spencer said, "You look fantastic."

"Thank you. So do you."

Spencer smiled. "Thanks. Are you ready to go?"

"Let me get my purse and my wrap and I will be."

Georgie's dress was one she'd bought for an event that was canceled so she'd never worn it. The dress had a fitted, high-necked, silver jeweled bodice over royal-blue chiffon with a chiffon floor-length skirt of the same royal blue. The back was low cut with the same jeweled straps crisscrossed over it.

The wrap she'd bought to go with it wasn't terribly warm, but then she wouldn't be out in the cold for long. And tonight wasn't extremely cold anyway. When she'd seen the shawl—a silver gossamer with blue shot through it— she'd known instantly she had to have it for her dress.

Interestingly, she'd found it in Whiskey River, at Fallen Angels of all places.

She'd wondered why a lingerie shop would carry a shawl and Chantel, one of the owners, had laughed. "We went on a buying trip and both of us loved it," she'd told Georgie. "We do that sometimes, pick up something that isn't lingerie. Our customers like to see the quirky things we come up with."

"I wouldn't call this quirky," Georgie had said. "It's gorgeous."

"True, but the quirkiness lies in the fact that it's for sale in a lingerie shop. We just put it out this morning."

"Must be kismet," Georgie had said. "I definitely want it. Now, about that lingerie." So of course, she'd had to buy a new set of lingerie to go underneath the dress and shawl.

The Christmas Ball benefitting the rodeo was held at Jameson House. The hospital's benefactress, Ruby Jameson, had willed the family home to the hospital and it housed several nonprofit organizations' offices. The huge Victorian-style house had a very large ballroom that was often used for events, particularly ones to benefit good causes.

Georgie had gotten the scoop about the place from Marcella but nothing her friend had told her had quite prepared Georgie for the Jameson House Ballroom decorated to the hilt for Christmas.

They walked into a winter wonderland. Tall, white birch trees, their bare branches strung with twinkling lights, formed an arch at the ballroom entrance. White-flocked Christmas trees with gold and silver balls were scattered throughout the room. Round tables were placed around the edge of the dance floor, complete with gleaming white tablecloths and festive centerpieces of scented votive candles in crystal holders set in a circle of snow-dusted pine cones and white flowers.

Long tables were set up along the sides of the room, loaded with all sorts of food. The focal point of each table was a silver reindeer wearing a red flower on its horns. Light entrees, hors d'oeuvres and desserts of every kind were arrayed on three-tiered serving platters clustered around the reindeer and fanning out among greenery lit with tiny twinkling lights.

The polished wood of the dance floor gleamed and the men's black tuxes and formal western tuxes contrasted with the sparkle and glitter of dresses in a thousand different colors and styles. She turned to Spencer who was watching her with a faint smile.

"Like it?" he asked.

"It's unbelievable. Like being in a fairy tale. Whoever was in charge of the decorations is a genius."

"There's a Christmas committee but the members change every year. It looks nice."

"Nice? It's absolutely gorgeous."

"So are you."

The way he looked at her made her breath catch in her throat. "Thank you. But I'm usually told I'm 'cute,'" she said, making a face.

"There's nothing wrong with being cute. Which you are, usually. Very cute. But tonight...tonight you're all-out gorgeous."

"I never thought I was terribly susceptible to flattery, but apparently I was wrong."

"It's not flattery when it's the truth," he answered, and led her onto the dance floor.

SO THEY DANCED. Spencer sensed a change in Georgie, which had begun when Cole had come into town. Seeing her ex-boyfriend had changed something for her. What, he wasn't sure. But she'd sworn she and Cole were through, so he meant to take her at her word.

When the band played a slow song he held her close and they danced silently for a while. Her cheek rested against his chest and he couldn't help wondering if this change he sensed in Georgie meant a change in their relationship. But he wasn't sure how to ask, or even whether he should ask.

About midway through the evening, when the band took a break, the president of the Daughters of Last Stand got up on the stage to make an announcement. "Thanks to the generosity of everyone here tonight, as well as some who couldn't make it to the ball, the Rodeo Scholarship is now fully funded. We truly appreciate all you do for the community."

Spencer and Georgie were alone for the moment, sitting at one of the tables. "I'm going to bring up the elephant in the room," Spencer said after the announcement.

"What elephant?"

"Cole. I was surprised not to see him here tonight. I didn't figure he'd give up on you so easily."

"I told you I was going to make sure he knew we were over. I saw him this morning. He didn't give up easily. He even offered to move here."

"Sounds serious." Shit, offering to move for her was a pretty damn big deal.

She laughed. "He'd hate it here. And even if he didn't, he'd resent me for making him move. I told him so, and that it was too late and we were done. He believed me finally and left."

"He just accepted that?"

"I also told him I'd moved on."

Spencer snorted in disgust. "Yeah, with me, your pretend boyfriend."

"No, I admitted that wasn't true." She looked him in the eye, a faint smile on her lips. "But I said we were headed that way. At least, I hoped we were."

Caught completely off guard, Spencer stared at her. "You did? I mean, you do?"

"Yes."

"Why did you change your mind?"

She shrugged. "Seeing Cole again made me realize that our relationship didn't succeed for many reasons. Working together wasn't a problem—until we broke up. And while I'm still a little hesitant given what happened with Cole, it seemed like a poor reason not to even give us a chance. Even though I work with you, I can't deny my feelings about you any longer. Denial doesn't make them go away, or change them."

"What kind of feelings?"

"I like you. I like you a lot."

"Come with me," he said, and grabbed her hand. He walked out of the ballroom and looked around for a private or at least semiprivate place to talk to her. He found an unoccupied room that looked like an old-fashioned parlor and pulled her inside with him.

"Define 'I like you a lot.'"

Georgie laughed and put her arms around his neck. "You're pretty smart. I bet you can figure it out."

"Humor me."

She kissed him. Her lips were soft and giving. Her tongue danced inside his mouth, asking his to play. Spencer groaned and wrapped his arms around her. He was drowning in her. In her sweet scent, and her spicy taste, tantalizing and uniquely hers. She was liquid fire in his arms, flames boosting his blood close to the boiling point. Fortunately, before he exploded on the spot, she ended the kiss.

"Does that answer your question?"

"I don't know. I think I need a deeper explanation."

"I believe that can be arranged."

"Now?"

"Oh, no," she said, shaking her head. "You promised me a date and it's still early. Let's go dance."

He grinned at her. "If that's what you want, then lead on."

They danced. They ate, feeding each other bites of food. They talked, about everything from sports to books. And then they danced some more. In between sets they talked to friends, but Spencer only half paid attention. No, his mind was all on Georgie. Finally the night wound down and they went home.

Spencer pulled into his parking space at the apartments. Before they got out he said, "Georgie, I don't want to move too fast. If you ask me to come to your apartment that doesn't mean—"

"Yes."

"You haven't let me finish."

"You don't need to."

"I think I do. I didn't ask you to come to the Christmas Ball with me expecting to get lucky. I wasn't even sure you were going to go with me. And I wasn't sure you were really done with Cole. So don't feel—I don't want you to think I expect…anything." God, he was messing this up. You'd think he'd never been with a woman before. But he hadn't been with Georgie. And he knew if they did make love it would be important. That it wouldn't be like it had been with other women. He'd liked them. Cared about them. Just as they'd cared about him. But not enough to make it special.

Georgie was special.

"Are you finished?"

"I guess."

"That was very sweet. And quite unnecessary."

"Why?"

"Because it's like you said in Whiskey River. Given half a chance we can't keep our hands off each other." She leaned over and kissed him. A kiss of promise and temptation. "Come to my apartment," she whispered.

"Anything you want, Georgie."

Chapter Thirteen

WHEN THEY WALKED inside her apartment Georgie tossed her keys and purse on a small table by the door. Then she draped her wrap over the back of a chair. She turned and smiled at him. "Do you want something to drink?"

"No. I'm good."

"Do you want to take off your coat and stay awhile?"

He laughed. "I didn't want to be pushy." He took off his jacket and tossed it over another chair.

"You're not. In fact, you couldn't be less pushy."

He walked over to her and framed her face in his hands. He kissed her, slow and sure and deep. Then he leaned his forehead against hers. "I told you before, I didn't expect to get lucky. So I'm not prepared. Which means if we're headed where I think—and hope—we're headed I need to make a trip to my apartment."

"I'm way ahead of you."

"You are?"

She put her arms around his neck and tugged his head down for a kiss. A hot kiss that nearly blasted his control to shreds. "I stopped by the drugstore this afternoon, after I saw

Cole. That's when I decided I shouldn't deny something we both want simply because I was too afraid to risk being hurt again. No risk, no gain." She began undoing the buttons on his shirt. "Don't you agree?"

"Hell, yes." While she undid the buttons, he took out his cuff links and tossed them on the coffee table. As soon as she'd unbuttoned enough of his shirt, he yanked it off over his head. Then he picked her up and carried her to her bedroom. Once there, he set her on her feet and took her in his arms. "But I'm not planning to hurt you." He slanted his lips over hers, claiming her mouth with his. She was soft and pliant in his arms. He ran his hands up her back, feeling the smooth, silky skin left bare by her dress.

"I need some help," she said, turning her back to him and brushing her hair out of the way. "This dress is hard to get out of."

"I'm sure I can be of use." But he couldn't figure out where to undo it. There was a zipper, but that was to the skirt. How the hell did this thing come undone? He saw her shoulders shake and knew she was laughing at him. "Very funny, smart-ass. I don't have a clue how this works."

"There are hooks on the fabric at the neck."

"Could've fooled me." But now that she'd told him he found the small hooks hidden among the jeweled fabric and carefully undid them. Once those were open, she let the straps slide off her shoulders leaving her back completely bare. Which must mean…

Georgie turned around and he sucked in his breath. Georgie's breasts were beautiful. Pale skin, full breasts with pink-tipped nipples, pearling with her excitement.

"Spencer?" she said when he didn't move.

"Sorry, I was staring at perfection."

"Maybe you should do more than look."

"No maybe about it." He cupped her breasts, running his thumbs over the nipples. She made an *mmm* sound. He bent his head down and captured one nipple, licking and sucking it until it stood up in a tight nub. He bent her back over his arm and moved to the other breast, giving it the same treatment.

She straightened, reached behind her back and unzipped the dress, stepping out of it carefully, leaving her wearing silver high heels and a tiny pair of silver panties to match the shoes. "Damn, Georgie, if I'd known what you had on beneath that dress—" He broke off because he couldn't think straight. All he knew was how much he wanted her.

"Pretty, aren't they?" She reached for him, for the waistband of his slacks and undid them, pushing them over his hips and down his legs. He toed off his shoes, stepped out of the slacks and quickly shed the rest of his clothes.

He tumbled her onto the bed, landing between her legs with nothing but the very tiny sliver of fabric between his aching cock and her. Not wanting it to be over too quickly, he slid off her and caressed and sucked her breasts again, then worked his way down her body with his lips. He slipped one hand beneath her panties, sliding a finger inside where she was hot, wet and waiting for him. He teased her, sliding his fingers in and out of her, rubbing the aching bundle of nerves with his thumb.

"Condoms?" he asked hoarsely.

She pushed him onto his back and climbed on top of him to get to the bedside table. The movement put her breasts even with his mouth, so he indulged himself again. She gasped and moaned and then slid off of him, holding out a condom. "Me? Or you?"

"Better let me." As it was, he was unsure of his control. It had been a while for him and if Georgie put the condom on him any restraint he had managed to maintain would be blasted to bits. She grinned and rolled onto her back. Bending her knee, she propped her opposite foot on it and slowly undid her sandal, tossing it away. Then she repeated the process with the other one. Damn, who knew how sexy it would be to watch a woman take off her shoes? Georgie made it into an art form.

She started to take off her panties, but he stopped her. "No, let me." He hooked his fingers in the elastic on the sides and began to draw them down her legs, slowly. He followed with his lips until he'd pulled them all the way down and tossed them after her shoes. He smiled at her from his vantage point at her feet, and strung kisses up her leg until he reached the apex of her thighs. She reached for him but he shook his head and parted her thighs, then used his mouth to bring her to a shattering climax.

As soon as she came he thrust his shaft inside her, and pumped in and out in deep thrusts. She raised her hips to meet him stroke for stroke until she spasmed around him and he came endlessly, spilling deep inside her.

AFTER THEY CLEANED up they both got back in bed. For a long time Spencer simply held her, kissing her mouth and her neck occasionally, and cuddling her close. They didn't really talk but it was a comfortable silence. "Do you want me to leave?" he asked her after a while. His hand was busy playing with her breasts at the time so she figured he didn't mean it.

"No. Do you want to leave?"

"No. But I wanted to make sure you were okay with me staying."

"I want you to stay."

"Good." He kissed her and tucked her in close to him. "Georgie?"

"Spencer?" she repeated in the same questioning tone.

He laughed at that. "Have I told you how glad I am that you changed your mind about us?"

"You didn't exactly tell me. But I got the picture." They'd been spooning, her back to his front, but now she turned around and looped her arms around his neck. "I'm glad too." His eyes were a deep green. Not hazel, but green. Really beautiful and unusual eyes. But then, the whole man was beautiful. And certainly not ordinary.

"I've been thinking about this, about making love to you, for a long time now," Spencer said.

"We haven't known each other that long."

"Yes, but I've been dreaming about this since I met you."

"Hmm. I spent all that time trying *not* to think about

you and me. And what would happen if we got together. But if I'd known—" she kissed him "—what this would be like I'd never have resisted as long as I did."

He smiled, flipped her on her back, and started working his way down her body, one kiss at a time. She allowed it for a little while but then tugged on his hair—silky dark blond and messed up from her hands—and said, "My turn." Then she pushed him onto his back and kissed her way down his body. "Looks like you're happy to see me," she murmured when she reached his cock, now standing at full attention.

"You have no idea," he said, and put his hands in her hair while she blew his mind, among other things.

⚜

WHAT'S BUZZING? SPENCER cracked open an eye. His phone. He grabbed it and looked at the time first. Seven freaking a.m.? Then the readout. Fred? Why would Fred be calling him at the crack of dawn on a Sunday morning?

He got out of bed and left the room, closing the door carefully behind him so he wouldn't wake Georgie. After last night she needed her sleep. He looked around in her living room, smiling at his clothes—jacket tossed over a chair, tie and shirt tossed on the floor.

"Fred?"

"Spencer?"

His voice was quivery and he sounded like he was about a hundred and ten. "Yes. What's wrong, Fred?" He found his tux shirt with half the buttons still fastened. He'd been in too much of a hurry last night to deal with them. He undid the rest of them and shrugged into it, but the rest of his clothes were in the bedroom where Georgie slept.

"Nothing's wrong. Exactly."

Great. Fred always said that same phrase when something was wrong but he didn't really want to talk about it. Spencer was his go-to guy in those situations. But his comment also meant Spencer would have to drag whatever had happened out of him. "Hold on a minute. And do not hang up." He put down the phone and entered the bedroom, gathering up his clothes as quietly as he could. He needn't have worried. Georgie was still asleep, dead to the world. Well, she was a paramedic. She could probably sleep through anything, except the tones, of course. No, those warning tones would wake any firefighter or EMS person up instantly.

He closed the bedroom door carefully behind him, picked up the phone and held it between his ear and shoulder so he could yank on his boxers and slacks. "Tell me what's wrong, Fred," he said as he redressed. He squelched the urge to tell him to get to the point. He never did.

"Well, I took me a drive this morning," Fred said, sounding a little stronger. "Along about an hour ago. Thought I'd go see some of them Christmas decorations over in Whiskey River."

Christmas decorations at six in the morning? Oh, well, that was no more odd than any number of things Fred had been doing lately.

"So I was driving along but it was takin' a long time to

get there. I've been there before, you know. Probably a hundred times. Didn't think it was that far away."

Oh, no. "It's not. Where are you, Fred?"

"That's the thing. I don't know."

Crap. He was going to have to go get him. But he had to find him first.

This was the second time that Spencer knew of that Fred had driven somewhere and gotten lost. There were undoubtedly other times he didn't know about. He hadn't discussed it with Fred's daughter, Honor, because Fred had begged him not to. Now he wished he'd ignored the old man and talked to Honor anyway.

He sat to put on his shoes and socks while Fred rambled about Whiskey River and how it could have moved from where it used to be. Then he grabbed his jacket, checked to make sure he had his keys, saw his cuff links on the coffee table and grabbed them, and started to leave. At the last minute he remembered he should leave a note for Georgie.

"Hold on a minute." He looked around the kitchen, found a scrap of paper and a pen, scribbled a note for her, and stuck it to the refrigerator door with a magnet.

"Okay," he said, walking out her apartment door. "Are you still there?"

"I'm here. Don't know where, though."

"Do you know what road you're on? Are you on Highway 290?"

"No, I was but I turned off that a while back."

"Did you go east or west on 290?"

"West, o' course," he said scornfully.

Well there was a big part of the problem. He should have been going east on 290 to go to Whiskey River.

"What road did you turn onto? Big? Small? Two lane?"

"It was kinda small—damn, I can't remember the number. Seventy-three? Sixteen? No, it wasn't sixteen. Maybe it was thirty-seven."

Other than Highway 16 he didn't remember any of those numbers being anywhere nearby. "Let me get this straight. You went west on Highway 290 out of town."

"I guess so."

Spencer tried not to grit his teeth. "Let's try this. Where did you start from?"

"My apartment, of course."

Fred lived in Last Stand's fairly new senior independent living apartment complex on the north side of town. "And you went west on 290, right?" he repeated.

"Said I did, didn't I?"

"And you turned off of it when? Had you been gone a long time when you got off the highway?"

"A while," Fred agreed.

"I'll call you when I get closer. In the meantime, stay where you are. Do not go anywhere."

"But I—"

"Promise me you'll stay put."

"Oh, all right," Fred said.

Spencer went to his apartment and threw on jeans, a shirt and running shoes, grabbing his leather jacket and a couple of bottles of water on his way out. Half an hour after he first got the phone call, Spencer had a general idea of where Fred had gone. Nowhere near Whiskey River, that's for sure. No, Fred had driven off in the opposite direction. Spencer headed west on 290, praying that at least that much was right. The only landmark Fred remembered seeing was a stand of trees before his very last turn. But first Spencer had to find the road he'd turned onto when he left 290. The trees marked yet another turn.

"I'll be there as soon as I can. Don't leave, okay?" he repeated. "Stay put so I can find you."

"Well, okay, but I could probably get out to that main road."

And get lost again. "No, just stay there, Fred. I'll be there to get you soon."

※

GEORGIE WOKE SLOWLY, stretched and looked at the pillow next to her. Spencer wasn't there. The only thing left of him was an indentation where his head had rested. She thought about the night before, savoring it. Last night had been special. The sex had been amazing but there'd been more. A connection she'd never felt with anyone else. How could that be after knowing each other such a short time?

What's right is right.

Maybe Spencer had made coffee, though she didn't smell any. He was resourceful enough to find the makings in her apartment. She rolled out of bed and grabbed clothes—a T-shirt, panties and pajama pants out of her drawers. Sure, she could have gone looking for him naked but their relationship was too new for her to feel comfortable doing so.

She wandered into her den and kitchen but she knew Spencer wasn't there. The apartment had an empty vibe to it. Maybe he'd gone out to buy coffee rather than bother making it. Since she was in dire need of caffeine, she sincerely hoped so. She checked her cell but there were no missed calls or messages.

She realized there was a note on her refrigerator, stuck up there with one of her magnets. She hadn't noticed right off, since there were several other things papering the surface, stuck beneath magnets. Spencer's note was short and not a bit sweet.

Something came up I had to take care of. Sorry. I'll call you later. S

Typical male, she thought. Something came up. How informative. It reminded her of a couple of times Cole disappeared after a night together. At least Spencer had left a note. Those two times Cole hadn't even managed that. Of course, he'd apologized profusely and she'd forgiven him, but it still rankled. And the memory still hurt.

And why was she thinking about Cole when she'd just spent the most amazing night of her life with Spencer? So what if he had to leave? That didn't necessarily mean anything was wrong.

She was paranoid, that's all. Who could blame her after what happened the last time she got involved with someone she worked with? Spencer—

Well, she didn't know if he felt the same as she did about

the night before, or if they had a future but she wanted to give the two of them a chance to find out.

After making and drinking her coffee, Georgie showered and got dressed, did some wash, stopped by the grocery store, and cleaned her apartment, even though it didn't need cleaning. In all that time her phone didn't ring once. Not. One. Time. So much for Spencer's "I'll call you later." When? Next week?

But what if something really awful had happened? To one of his family members? Then she'd feel terrible for being mad at him. There were a number of scenarios that would give him a perfectly good reason for not letting her know something sooner.

Right. And then there's the one where he totally forgot about you.

After last night?

Who's to say he isn't accustomed to mind-blowing sex?

But last night was special. For both of us.

Are you sure about that?

And the answer to that was a big old no.

Chapter Fourteen

ALTHOUGH HE KNEW the general direction Fred had gone Spencer made slow progress. First he had to find the road Fred had turned onto from Highway 290. He said he'd turned right and seemed pretty sure about that. But Fred never did figure out the number of that highway or road. Spencer didn't start looking for the first turnoff in earnest until he was about thirty minutes away from Last Stand, as Fred had been positive he'd been driving at least that long before he turned.

"This is stupid," he said aloud when he was about forty-five minutes out of town. "I'm going to have to call Sean Highwater to ping Fred's phone." He didn't want to because that would mean police reports, paperwork, and Fred's daughter being told. Of course, Fred didn't know it, but this time Spencer wasn't keeping quiet. It was too dangerous for the old man to drive anymore and his daughter would have to lay down the law. He suspected he would need to back her up, too. Something he wasn't looking forward to.

Shortly before he was ready to give up and call Sean, Spencer found a Highway 783. Given that Fred had mentioned both a seven and a three, he figured that was his best shot at the actual road.

But once on CR 783 he had to take every little road off of it that had a stand of trees marking it. He gave it a few more miles, turned off onto another tiny road marked by a copse, and hit the jackpot. Fred's red pickup sat just where he'd said it was. Fred had suggested more than once that he pull out to the main road, but Spencer had been afraid Fred would decide to drive off again and then he'd never find him.

He pulled up beside the pickup, parked his truck and got out. Fred hadn't moved from the driver's seat. Spencer wondered if the old man had even seen him. He rapped on the window and opened Fred's door. "Fred?" He put his hand on Fred's shoulder and squeezed gently. "Are you okay?"

"Spencer? What are you doing here?"

"You called me. Don't you remember?"

"I did? Why did I do that? I was on my way to Whiskey River."

"You got lost."

"I did? Are you sure?"

"I'm sure. How are you feeling?" He didn't look good but there could be any number of reasons for that.

"Not so good."

"Not good or bad? Did you just start feeling this way or have you been feeling bad for a while?" Great. What if he was having a heart attack? Or God knows what else it could be. Problem was, it could be something that needed immediate attention, in which case they could be screwed since he didn't know how far away the EMS team who covered this area was.

"Not long. Now don't you go thinking it's something bad. I don't feel real good, that's all. I could use some water, though."

"I've got some in the truck." He could be dehydrated. That was not uncommon in older people. On his way to get water, Spencer called 911. With no equipment there wasn't much Spencer could do for Fred unless he was forced to give him CPR, which he devoutly hoped he wouldn't be. Unless EMS was too far away, then he'd find out where the nearest hospital was and take Fred himself. It could be nothing to worry about, but Spencer wasn't taking any chances.

Fred would undoubtedly bitch about him calling EMS, but too bad.

"What'd you do that for?" Fred asked when he told him EMS was coming. "You're a damn paramedic. You can take care of me."

"Sorry, no I can't. I don't have any instruments or equipment. Don't worry, they'll be here soon. In the meantime, drink your water. I'm calling Honor."

"Oh, fer God's sake. Don't call her. She'll pitch a fit."

"Better Honor have a fit than be mad at me."

"You're scared of a little woman like Honor?" Fred asked scornfully.

"Damn straight I am. And so are you."

Fred couldn't argue that so he quit talking. Which was just fine with Spencer. He called Honor and gave her what details he could, promising to call when he knew what hospital they were going to and where it was.

When the paramedics came Spencer knew one of them, having gone through paramedic training with her. To be safe, they took Fred to a nearby hospital. But their diagnosis was what Spencer had thought it would be. Dehydration and hypoglycemia. Not, thank God, a heart attack.

GEORGIE'S CELL RANG about four-thirty and for a moment she thought it was Spencer. But then she realized it was Marcella's ringtone. She debated not answering but decided she might as well talk to her friend now rather than later.

"Hello."

"Hey, Georgie. Inquiring minds want to know. Did anything happen with Spencer? You two looked awfully cozy at the ball."

"What happened is I'm a fool."

"You sound upset."

"You could say that."

"Want to talk about it?"

Swallowing the lump in her throat, she said, "No." But then the whole story came pouring out. Marcella listened and made appropriate sounds of sympathy. Eventually, Georgie ran down. "Do you think I'm wrong to be upset? If it wasn't such a classic blow-off gesture I might not be."

"It could be," Marcella said, sounding unsure. "But he could have a good reason too. Did you try to call him?"

"Yes. His phone went to voice mail. And he didn't call

back."

"I see why you're upset and I don't blame you. But maybe he had a family emergency. Or maybe he got called in to work."

"I know and you could be right. But you'd think he'd manage to make a simple phone call or send a damn text."

"True. It does seem like he could have done that."

"I really didn't think Spencer was the slam, bam, thank you ma'am type of guy. I mean, we work together. Doesn't he realize how uncomfortable that's going to be if he blows me off? Or does he just not care?"

"Well, he's a male. You know they sometimes don't realize they're pissing you off. Not to be sexist, but sometimes men are just clueless."

Georgie snorted. "You can say that again."

"Why are you being so quick to judge him? Seriously, he could have a very good reason."

"Sure he could. And maybe he simply decided that I wasn't worth bothering with."

"Oh, come on, Georgie. That really doesn't sound like Spencer. What else is going on? Why would you think that?"

She could be overreacting. But she couldn't help how this made her feel. "Cole did that to me a couple of times. He apologized and after the second time when I got really upset he didn't do it again. But it made me feel—" She paused and then finished, "It made me feel like I didn't matter."

"Oh, Georgie, I'm sure Spencer didn't mean for you to feel this way. Give him a chance to explain."

Her other line beeped in. She pulled the phone away from her ear. "Speak of the devil. Guess who's on the other line?"

"See, I told you he'd call. I'll let you go."

Do not jump down his throat. Give him a chance to explain.

IT WAS AFTER five p.m. by the time Spencer managed to call Georgie. He was in his truck headed to the ranch to pick up someone to bring Fred's truck home. He figured Georgie would be pissed at him but he also knew that once he explained what had happened she'd forgive him. Still, he felt bad for having to leave her as he did after their night together. Their *first time* together. He hadn't planned to spend that day chasing Fred all over Hell and half of Georgia.

He wasn't quite finished with Fred. Just as he'd feared, Honor had asked him to be there to back her up when she told Fred he could no longer drive. It was the last thing he wanted to do but Honor didn't have anyone closer to the family than he was. As Georgie had pointed out at the market, Fred was as much a grandparent to him as his blood relatives had been.

He knew what a difficult decision it was to have to take someone's independence away from them. For that's what driving was to the older people he knew. It didn't matter that there was a bus for the senior independent living apartments that Fred lived in to take him wherever he needed to go. The fact that he could no longer get in his car and do whatever he wanted to do whenever he wanted to do it would be a crushing blow to him, as it would be to most older people. His own grandparents had passed a long time ago, but Spencer still remembered the battle that had raged when his mom had to take away her dad's keys.

And because he remembered that he had no choice but to be there for Honor and Fred.

He was meeting Honor and Fred at Fred's apartment once he was discharged from the hospital. In the meantime, he had to explain to Georgie why he'd left the way he had.

The phone rang several times before she picked up. "Hello."

"I thought you weren't there or weren't answering," Spencer said. "I was about to leave a message."

"I'm here."

He plunged right into it. "I'm sorry I had to leave like I did. You're not going to believe what happened. Early this—"

She interrupted before he could finish his sentence. "Is everything all right?"

"Yes, the crisis has been taken care of. Mostly, anyway."

"I assumed it was since you managed to call me. Was it your family?"

"No, not exactly. It was—"

"Was it work-related?"

"No, it was—"

"Save it."

"It wasn't family but let me tell you—"

"No need. Something important happened and you

didn't have time to call or text. All you had time for was a lousy note that said nothing. I get it."

Yeah, she was pissed. "Look, I've still got something I have to do but after that I'll be free. Can I come over and bring some food and explain everything to you?"

"Sorry. I'm busy washing my hair," she said sarcastically. "Maybe some other time. Like, oh, how about never?"

"Georgie, I wouldn't have left if it hadn't been important."

"I don't doubt that."

"You sure sound like you do."

"Let me ask you something. Was this crisis life and death?"

"No. But I wasn't sure what it was at the time."

"But once you knew, you couldn't manage a phone call or a text at some point during the day? Just a quick message to give me some idea why you ran out of here the morning after the night we spent together? Something came up? That was it?"

Spencer scrubbed a hand over his face. Yes, in hindsight he should have given her a little more explanation but he'd been in a hurry. And yes, he shouldn't have waited until so late to even get in touch. But he'd been worried about Fred, worried he wouldn't find him before the old man took off again. And later, with EMS and the hospital and calling Honor... Well, he'd thought about it but he put it off because he wanted to talk to her. Which, upon reflection, was stupid. But all that was hindsight. "I should have called you earlier. I'm sorry, but it's been crazy."

"That's fine," she said in a tone that meant it was anything but fine. "I'm glad everything is all right. I've got to go," she said and the line went dead.

Shit. He'd really blown it.

Chapter Fifteen

THE FOLLOWING DAY Georgie worked with Marcella. Spencer was firefighting again, which she thought was just as well. She alternated between being curious about Spencer's excuse for not calling her and telling herself that it didn't matter and she was glad she'd found out early on how undependable he was.

Except she didn't really think he was undependable. So reconciling what had happened—Spencer totally forgetting about her—with the fact that she knew him to be a stand-up guy didn't make a lot of sense.

Her other problem was that she kept remembering their night together and how amazing it had been. Damn it.

"Did you ever find out what happened with Spencer?" Marcella asked when she saw her.

"Not exactly."

"He didn't tell you? What did he say?"

Georgie looked around but they were alone in the galley. "He said that everything was okay and that it had been crazy. Oh, and it wasn't anyone in his family. And it wasn't work related."

"That's all he said? Are you kidding?" Marcella poured a

cup of coffee. "Want one?"

"Sure. Thanks." She took a sip and said, "Once I found out it wasn't his family and it wasn't life or death, or work, I told him to save it."

"You didn't even let him explain? Don't you think that was kind of harsh? Those three things aren't the only good excuses."

"Maybe not, but they cover a lot of ground. So no, I don't think it's at all harsh. I thought the fact that he didn't even think to text me was a pretty good indication of where I stand with him." Noticing Marcella was frowning at her she said, "You think I'm being a bitch."

"No. But I think you might regret being mad at him without hearing him out."

Irritated, because Marcella was only voicing what she herself had been wondering, she snapped, "I don't need to hear him out to know when I'm being blown off. And what's with you defending him?"

"Now you're being bitchy," Marcella said mildly, observing her over the rim of her coffee cup.

Georgie stared at her with her mouth open. She closed her eyes and mumbled, "Damn it." She looked at her friend. "You're right. I'm sorry. I'm obviously more upset than I thought I was." She couldn't help laughing. "But trust you to tell me the truth."

"Hey, what are friends for?"

Shortly after that they went out on a call, but Marcella had given her a lot to think about in a very short time. Maybe she was being too hard on Spencer. She could be overreacting because of what had happened with Cole. She'd forgiven Cole and they'd moved past it, but she'd never been able to forget the way it had made her feel. Plus, the fact that Cole would never commit to her—until after they broke up, anyway—hadn't helped her get over her hurt feelings.

Because that's what it was, basically. Spencer had hurt her feelings, almost certainly unintentionally. And in effect, she was making Spencer pay for Cole's faults. She was being a baby—or a bitch, take your pick—to not even let him explain. After her shift was over early that Christmas Eve morning she looked for him, but he'd already left. She called and left a message on his phone to please call her back.

He didn't.

Since today was Christmas Eve, it was the day they had the party to pass out the gifts from the toy drive for the kids. She knew Spencer would be busy with that. And so would she. She couldn't abandon her commitment to the toy drive just because she and Spencer had a misunderstanding. The party was from three to four-thirty, to give everyone plenty of time to get home to their families on Christmas Eve night. Georgie had promised her own family she'd go to Fort Worth for Christmas Day, but for tonight she was all alone.

She needed to make amends with Spencer. She'd have to corner him at the party. Not a great place to have any sort of private discussion but it couldn't be helped. At the least she could convince him to talk to her after the party.

Unless he was so mad at her that he wouldn't even talk to her.

IN PREPARATION FOR the party, the fire engines, trucks, and other vehicles had been moved out of the bay. They were still ready to go for any emergency but there was always a chance that no emergencies would require their help during the several hours before, during and after the party when their guests would be there.

He glanced around, thinking there must be even more volunteers than usual this year. Everyone from emergency services and the fire department who could manage it were there. The Daughters of Last Stand were all there, of course, since the toy drive was one of their community projects. They took care of setting up the food, drinks, and organizing the gifts into age groups and names so it would be easier to find them. Other people were busy putting up decorations. Not including mistletoe, he was happy to see. Since it was a kids' party the decision had been made to forego the mistletoe.

Mistletoe reminded him of Georgie. Spencer couldn't decide if he was more upset with himself or with Georgie. Honestly, he acknowledged they were both at fault. But was he going to let a stupid misunderstanding ruin what he believed he could have with Georgie?

It was way too soon for Spencer to be thinking of settling down with Georgie. Except he was thinking about it. Or he had been before she blew him off. He'd really thought she could be "the one." But when she wouldn't even listen to him he'd decided maybe he was wrong.

Yet her reaction seemed like an overreaction to him. What had happened to make her respond the way she had? I mean, yeah, he should have called sooner but damn it, he'd had about all he could do to take care of Fred until Honor could get to the hospital. It pissed him off that Georgie was being so unreasonable, so when she called and left him a message he'd ignored it.

Which was probably—okay, definitely—stupid and childish.

Georgie had been avoiding him, just as he'd avoided her. But she came over to him shortly before the party was to start. "I tried to call you earlier," she said.

"Yeah, I know. I've been busy." At the moment he wasn't doing a damn thing, which she could obviously see.

"Can we talk about what happened?"

"You mean how you blew me off when I tried to explain why I had to leave?"

She pressed her lips together, as though trying to keep herself from saying something. But she only said, "Yes."

"Now isn't a good time."

"I know. But I wanted to catch you before the party was over and you left. Can we talk afterward?"

He shrugged, as if it wasn't important. "Sure."

"Good." She left and he stared after her. So she was ready to listen. But was he ready to explain?

The party was a success, as it always was. The Christmas tree was lit up and looked pretty good, if you didn't consider the angel on the top that listed to the side and had seen better days. There was tinsel everywhere, which meant they'd be finding it in strange places for months. The food was displayed on colorful paper plates sporting classic Christmas pictures. Santa and his elves and reindeer, poinsettias, Christmas trees, snowmen. There was every kind of plate and plastic cups to go with them. Not that he thought the kids cared, but the women were always adamant that the party tableware be properly decorative.

The looks on the kids' faces when they opened their presents were priceless.

Even the teenagers among them were excited, though they tried to be too cool to show it. But their happiness couldn't be hidden.

It was also as usual, a madhouse. With the volunteers, the children, their parents, and a random assortment of others, there was a mass of people there. And once the presents were opened—watch out. But eventually the party wound down, leaving him, Georgie, and some of the other volunteers to clean up. Someone, and he hoped it was a kid, had stuffed several cupcakes in the Christmas tree stand. He had no idea why, but there it was. Since the tree was artificial and would be stored for another year, it would need to be cleaned before that could happen. Getting the cupcake and icing out meant he wound up with his arm being covered in icing up to his shoulder.

While he was washing up Georgie came over to him. "You look like you bathed in icing."

"I almost did. I was cleaning the tree. If I don't do it now it might get stored that way. And trying to get year-old icing and cake out of the stand is damned near impossible. I've tried before."

"Can we talk now?"

"Okay." Wanting to see what she said, he didn't respond further.

"Somewhere a little more private?"

He shrugged. "Whatever you say."

She led him inside the station, into an empty office.

"Let me have it," he said when she closed the door.

She turned around, a shocked expression on her face. "You think I'm going to yell at you?"

"The thought crossed my mind, yeah."

"I'm not. I want—I need—Oh, shit. I'm trying to apologize."

He started to speak but she hushed him. "Let me finish. Please. I overreacted Sunday and got mad at you when I shouldn't have. I'm sure you had a good reason for what happened. I should have let you explain. Instead I went off on you."

"You mean for leaving you so early with only a *lousy note* in explanation?"

She frowned at him. "Yes. You have to admit the note basically said nothing."

"It's all I had time for." He could see she was struggling. God, he hoped she wouldn't start crying. He'd be toast if she did that. "Fred called. He'd driven somewhere and gotten lost. I had to go find him and I was afraid he'd take it into his head to start driving again and God knows where he'd have gone. As it was I had the devil of a time finding him."

"Fred? The Fred you play dominoes with every Tuesday?"

"Yeah."

"I asked you if it had been family who needed you and you said no."

"He's not family. Technically."

"Don't be ridiculous. He's as good as family. I wish you'd told me."

"Are you saying you wouldn't have been mad if I'd told you I was going to help Fred?"

"Of course not. I know you think of him like family."

Well, damn. He should have given her more credit. "I should have called you some time during the day but I kinda had my hands full."

"I wish you'd told me," she repeated.

"Why did you get so pissed? I mean, yeah, it was stupid of me not to give you some idea of what was going on, but I thought you'd realize I'd never have left like I did if it hadn't been important."

"You mean why didn't I trust you?"

He shrugged. "Yeah."

"Prior experience."

"Cole."

"Yes, Cole. When we first started dating Cole did something similar to me. Except it wasn't important and he thought it wasn't a big deal. But it was. It made me feel shitty, and like I didn't matter. When you left like you did and didn't call or text all day I felt just like I did when Cole forgot about me."

He took a step until he stood very close to her. "Damn.

I'm sorry, Georgie. I should have called sooner."

"I'm sorry too. I feel like a fool."

He had to laugh at that. "I'm there with you. Why don't we agree we both could have handled it better?"

"That sounds good to me."

He touched her cheek with the backs of his fingers. "That night was special to me. You matter to me. You matter a lot."

Her gaze softened. "You matter to me too. A lot." She smiled. "Are we friends again?"

He pulled her into his arms. "I was hoping for a little more."

"Were you?" she asked, and kissed him.

He sat in one of the chairs and tugged on her hand so she'd sit in his lap. He kissed her, his tongue sweeping inside her mouth, tasting, testing, teasing. Wrapping her arms around his neck, she met his tongue with hers, thrust for thrust.

The door opened and a male voice said, "Get a room, people."

"Go away, Cable."

Cable laughed and shut the door.

They kissed some more and then Spencer regretfully called a halt. "We'd better go back and see what else needs to be done."

"Okay. Will I see you later?"

"I have something I need to do. It might take me a long time. Can I text you later?"

"Of course."

"You're not going to flip out if it's late, are you?"

She punched him in the arm, though lightly. "I'll try to control myself."

After they finished up and Georgie left, Spencer called Jethro Caldwell, the man who owned the ranch where he and Georgie had gotten stuck. The infamous ditch was also the site of their first kiss. Not counting the mistletoe kiss, anyway.

"Who's this?" the old man snapped by way of greeting.

"Hi, Mr. Caldwell. This is Spencer McBride."

"Spencer? Are you checking up on me? I went to the doctor," he said indignantly. "He said my hand is fine."

"I'm not calling about that."

"You're not?"

"No. I'm calling to ask you for a favor."

"What kind of a favor?" the old man asked suspiciously.

"I need some help romancing my girl."

Jethro cackled. "I can get behind that. What do you need, son?"

Chapter Sixteen

GEORGIE TRIED HER best not to worry while waiting for Spencer to call. She trusted him. Of course she did. Especially after their big talk and reconciliation. But what the hell could he be doing that was taking so long? Maybe he'd gone out to his parents' place. After all, it was Christmas Eve. But why hadn't he told her if that was it? Surely she knew she'd understand family commitments. She'd told him so when they talked about Fred. So if it was his family, why hadn't he texted?

Georgie answered her phone when she heard Marcella's ringtone. "Hi, Marcella."

"Hey. I'm headed out but I wanted to check on you. I'm guessing the fact that you and Spencer disappeared during cleanup—and didn't come back for quite a while—means you two made up."

"We did. We apologized to each other and both of us explained what had happened. So yes, we've made up," she said, remembering those kisses in the empty room at the station.

"What did he say happened?"

"Fred Appleblum got lost driving somewhere and Spencer had to find him. I gathered dealing with that kept him busy most of the day."

"Fred? The Fred who is like family to him?"

"The very same."

"I knew Spencer had a good reason. He really is a good guy, Georgie."

"I know. I can't tell you how stupid and bad I felt when he told me what he'd been doing all day. If he'd only told me it was Fred, I'd never have gotten mad. But he didn't. And as if that wasn't enough, right before I left the station, I saw Fred's daughter, Honor. She said that Spencer even helped her to convince Fred to give up his keys. She said she'd been dreading it and went on and on about how great Spencer is. You know how adamant people of Fred's generation are about driving. Anyway, Spencer talked to him too and by the end of it, Fred gave Honor his keys. Not happily, of course, but he did it."

"Spencer to the rescue," Marcella said with a sympathetic laugh.

"Yes. This is one more thing I didn't know and get to feel like a fool about. Why is Spencer so damn modest?"

"Just his nature, I guess." Marcella paused and added, "Spencer's not with you right now, is he?"

"Would I be telling you all this if he was? No, he's not here."

"Is he coming over later?"

"I don't know."

"I'm surprised he's not with you after what you told me. Where is he?"

"I don't know that either. But the one thing I do know is I'm not going to flip out about it if I don't hear from him."

"Sounds like a plan," Marcella said. "Good luck and let me know what happens."

Georgie piddled around for a bit and finally decided it was time for the big guns. She got out a spoon, then went to the freezer and pulled out the tub of chocolate chip ice cream. She'd bought it in a weak moment and had been trying not to eat it. But if anything called for ice cream, this situation did.

She took her ice cream into the living room and turned the TV on to *How the Grinch Stole Christmas*. Yes, she knew it was a kid's movie but it made her laugh and she figured she needed that right now. She'd polished off half of the tub and was feeling slightly sick when her phone rang again. It wasn't Spencer's ringtone but her pulse had picked up regardless the moment it rang.

"Hello."

"Is this Georgie Durant?"

"Yes. Who is this?"

"It's Jethro."

"Jethro?" she repeated blankly.

"Jethro Caldwell."

It took her a moment to remember who he was. "Mr. Caldwell? How did you get my phone number?"

"You gave it to me. Don't you remember when you came out here with Spencer?"

No, she didn't remember that. She supposed she could have. Or maybe he'd looked it up online. Or his granddaughter had. "Is something wrong, Mr. Caldwell?"

"Darn tootin' something's wrong. I can't find Spencer. Thought maybe he was with you."

"No, I'm sorry, he's not here. Did you try his phone?"

"Of course. He ain't answering and I called the station looking for him but they said they hadn't seen him and he wasn't working tonight."

"Did you ask EMS to come out?"

"Nope. Didn't want them. I wanted Spencer. But since I can't find him, you'll do. You seem to have some sense. For a medical type," he added.

"Me? I don't have any medical equipment with me, Mr. Caldwell. You should call EMS. I'm sure they'll send some-one—"

He cut her off. "You're a paramedic, aren't you?"

"Yes, but—"

"I have a first aid kit here. That'll work." When she still hesitated he added, "I'm alone here. No telling what will happen if you don't come out. Please, Georgie."

"All right." She squeezed the bridge of her nose. She did have a few instruments at home, like a home blood pressure machine, an EpiPen, a stethoscope, and a glucose test. She kept them in her car as a precaution in case something happened when she wasn't working. But she hadn't really expected to put them to use. She'd never had to before and she'd been carrying a kit with those items in her car ever since she got her paramedic license. "Can you give me some idea what's wrong?"

"Can't tell you over the phone. Just come."

That's helpful. Not. "I'll be there as soon as I can. But are you sure you don't want me to have EMS come? I'd come with them," she added.

"No ambulance. Nobody but you. Promise."

What in the hell is going on? "All right. I won't call EMS. I promise." It went against the grain but if she sent EMS out to the ranch he was just as likely to send them packing. And she didn't want to send her colleagues out on a pointless call—especially not on Christmas Eve. Still, she'd call it in if she found she needed them once she got there and evaluated Jethro. She only hoped Jethro wouldn't need immediate help, but the fact that he'd talked to her coherently on the phone made her hope the problem wasn't serious.

Georgie called Spencer and not surprisingly, got his voice mail. She left him a message letting him know what she was doing and asking him to call her when he got it. What was he doing that he couldn't answer his damn phone?

I am not going to be paranoid about this.

EVERYTHING WAS SET and as ready as Spencer could make it. Since he couldn't get cell phone reception on most of Jethro Caldwell's property, he couldn't call to check that Jethro had come through for him and Georgie was on her way out to the ranch. But Jethro had gotten a real kick out of playing a critical role in Spencer's romantic plans for the evening so he wasn't too worried. And he didn't believe there was any way that Georgie would turn down Jethro.

It had taken some doing, but Spencer had cleared a flat space beneath one of the huge oak trees and spread out a blanket. Fortunately, it wasn't raining, so they wouldn't get stuck in the ditch or have limbs falling on them because of the wind. There was a slight chance for a dusting of snow, but Spencer had lived in the Hill Country almost all his life and suspected he could count on one hand the times it had snowed significantly.

A small, pre-decorated potted Christmas tree sat beside the blanket. It had lights but he had no way to plug it in so the other decorations would have to do. He'd brought a couple of beers from one of their favorite microbreweries, rather than wine, since they both preferred it. And a box of homemade chocolate chip cookies he'd conned his mother into baking. God knows he wouldn't ask his sister, who could burn water. And while he could cook, he was no baker.

He'd parked his truck a bit up the road with its headlights shining on the scene he'd set, so Georgie would see it and stop. No point tempting fate and just asking to be stuck in the ditch, regardless of the fact that it was dry as a bone tonight. In his pocket there was a small, wrapped jewelry box. Not a ring, though he had looked at them and been surprised that the sight of engagement rings didn't send him into a panic. But even though by now Spencer was certain that Georgie was "the one," it was way too early to talk about marriage.

And the pièce de résistance, a sprig of mistletoe that he'd climbed a tree to cut. He didn't have anywhere to hang it, so he figured he'd hold it over her head. Now all he had to do was wait.

Not too much later he heard a car and walked up the hill to meet it. Georgie got out and said, "Spencer? What are you doing here? I thought Jethro couldn't find you."

"Tonight Jethro is giving Clara Perkins a run for her money. He played matchmaker for me."

"Matchmaker?" she repeated blankly. Then understanding dawned. "You set this up?"

"I did. With a little help from Jethro." He took her hand and tugged her forward to kiss her lightly. "Come on, I'll show you." He led her down the hill to the picnic area he'd set up.

"Oh, Spencer. It's lovely. And look at the tree!" She squatted down beside it. "Look at these tiny ornaments. It's adorable." She rose and turned around, bursting out laughing when she saw him holding the mistletoe over his head. "I suppose this means I have to kiss you."

"It's tradition."

She sighed, but he saw her lips twitch. "If I must." She put her arms around his neck and kissed him, taking her time, waiting until he, at least, was at full boil before she drew back.

He let her go so she could sit. He'd placed three lanterns around them to give off some light and he turned them on before going up the hill to cut off his headlights. When he returned she offered him one of the beers.

She took a sip and said, "You know this is my new favorite brand, right?"

He rolled his eyes. "We had some in Whiskey River. Of

course I remember. And—" He reached for the box of cookies and presented them to her with a flourish. "Homemade chocolate chip."

She took one, bit into it and gave a moan of pleasure. "Oh, my God. These are amazing. You bake cookies?"

"Alas, no. My culinary abilities are limited to meals at the station. No desserts." She polished off one and reached for another. "My mom made these. She doesn't cook a lot but what she makes is always great. Of course, I had to come clean before she agreed to bake them."

Georgie paused with the cookie halfway to her mouth. "Come clean?"

"I might have told her they were for my girl."

"Am I your girl?"

"I hope so. Otherwise I went to all this trouble for nothing."

"Come here," she said, crooking a finger.

He moved closer to her. "Yes?"

"You rock," she said, and kissed him.

"Mmm. Chocolate chip," he said when they drew apart.

Georgie laughed. They toasted each other, drank some beer, ate some more cookies and talked.

"If you're cold I can get another blanket," Spencer said. "Or we can sit in the truck."

"I'll take the blanket but no way am I sitting in the truck. I like it here."

He went and got the blanket and handed it to her. When she finished arranging it, he pulled the small, wrapped box out of his jacket pocket. "The bow is kinda smushed. I forgot about it when I put it in my pocket. Merry Christmas, Georgie."

Her expression was priceless. Equal parts shock and dismay. "Oh, my God," he said laughing. "You should see your face. You can relax, Georgie. It's not a ring."

"I didn't think it was," she said huffily.

"Liar."

"Okay, fine. You got me." She frowned at him. "But you have to admit it looks like a ring box."

"It does. But I thought a ring might be a little premature since we've only known each other for a month. Go ahead. Open it."

"I have a present for you but it's at my place. Obviously, I wasn't expecting to see you."

"The present, Georgie. Open the present."

She finished ripping off the paper and opened the box. "Oh, Spencer. I love them." She threw her arms around him and hugged him.

"They're mistletoe earrings," he said in case she couldn't tell. "They had them in gold but I noticed you usually wear silver so that's what I got."

"I do. I'm impressed you noticed." She finished putting them on and asked, "How do they look?"

"They look like I should kiss you." Suiting action to words, he cupped her cheek and kissed her.

"I want to see what they look like but I'm too lazy to go to my car to look in the mirror. Besides, I'm comfortable here. I'll have to look later."

He wrapped her in his arms and she leaned back against

him. They sat that way for a while, with him kissing her hair from time to time. "I fell for you the moment I saw you at the Corbyns' party."

She turned her head to look at him. "You mean when you ran into me?"

"More like we ran into each other. But no, before that."

"Really? Are you saying you engineered that first meeting under the mistletoe?"

"No, but I would have if I'd thought of it."

They sat there for a while longer until Spencer said, "I swear it's getting colder. Are you ready to go?"

"I guess. This was so sweet of you, Spencer. You've made me feel very special."

"You are special." He kissed her. "That's one of the reasons I love you."

"You love me? Like…"

"I'm in love with you."

She stared at him and her eyes filled with tears.

"Hey, no crying. Pretend I never said it."

"Are you kidding? I love you too, Spencer."

"In that case—" he kissed her "—what do you say we take this party someplace warmer?"

"Sounds like a great idea."

SPENCER FOLLOWED HER to her place. Since she had thought she was going to the Caldwells' to see Jethro, Georgie hadn't brought Spencer's Christmas present with her. She hoped he liked it. She'd found it purely by accident at the Ugly Christmas Sweater Store on Main Street.

They started kissing the moment they walked in her door, but she reluctantly pulled away. "Hold that thought."

"Why?"

"Because I have something for you and if you distract me now I might forget to give it to you." Besides, she wanted to see if he liked it.

"A present?"

"It's Christmas. Of course it's a present."

He smiled that engaging smile he had with the dimples he definitely knew how to employ. "I like presents."

"Have a seat. Unless you want something to drink."

"I'm good. I'll wait."

She left the room and came back with a gift she'd wrapped herself. She'd found the giftwrap—what else but mistletoe—at Yippee Ki Yay. They had a big bin of Christmas wrap. Most of it was western Christmas themed, of course. But she'd dug through and snared a roll of mistletoe wrap. At first she'd worried that she was carrying the mistletoe theme too far, but after Spencer gave her the earrings she'd decided she clearly wasn't.

She handed him the wrapped box. "I didn't want to wait until tomorrow. First of all because of these," she said, flicking her earrings. "But I told my family I'd go to Fort Worth tomorrow to see them. Since I'm working the twenty-sixth I'll be coming back that night, so it's a really quick trip." Georgie fidgeted a minute then took the plunge. "You probably have plans with your family, but I'd love for you to come with me."

"You want to take me to meet your family?" He'd been looking at the gift but at that he glanced up.

"If it wouldn't freak you out. But I totally get it if you don't want—"

"I'd love to come with you."

"You would? And it won't freak you out?" she repeated.

"We shouldn't spend our first Christmas Day apart. And no, it doesn't worry me. I'd like to meet your family."

"What about your family? Don't you have plans?"

"Yes, but they're fluid. In a family of people in the medical field, someone is always likely to be on call. Usually me. And then if one of the horses decides to foal or something happens to the cattle, that lets out Jessie and my mom. We're used to working around it."

He tore open the giftwrap, opened the box and took out a large snow globe—a Christmas scene. "Wow."

He didn't say anything else, just stared at it. Georgie rushed to say, "If you don't like it I can get another. I thought the couple kissing under the mistletoe would remind you of us." Still, he didn't speak. "Or I'll return it and get something else." Obviously she'd blown it this time.

"No, this is perfect. Thank you," he said, and kissed her.

"Really? You're not just saying that?"

"Of course not. When I was a kid my grandmother— she's gone now—my mother's mother had a Christmas snow globe collection. All different scenes. Some were music boxes that circled while the song played, some were globes that didn't move and only snowed if you turned them upside down. Sometimes only the insides moved when you wound them. There were globes with Santas and trees and elves and reindeer. Some were big, some were small and there was everything in between. Every time we went to her house at Christmas I'd spend hours playing with those things. So when she died—" he cleared his throat "—she left her collection to me."

"Oh, Spencer, I'm sorry. I didn't meant to make you sad."

He looked at her like she was crazy. "Are you kidding? It's perfect. It's a good memory. You couldn't have picked anything better."

"Oh, good. You had me worried. It has music too."

"Cool." He wound it up and set it on the table, laughing when he heard the song. "Truer words, Georgie."

"I thought so, too," she said to the tune of "All I Want For Christmas Is You."

Chapter Seventeen

Six Months Later

"SO WHAT'S THE occasion?" Audrey was lounging on Georgie's bed while Georgie pulled every single dress she owned out of her closet.

"I don't know. Spencer wouldn't tell me. He just said it was special but he's being very mysterious." She pulled out another dress to show to her friend. "What about this one? I wore it to something we both went to. I can't remember what though."

"Don't remind me. You look like a bag lady in that dress. No. Definitely no."

Georgie choked back a laugh. "Don't hold back, Audrey. Tell me what you really think."

Audrey grinned. "You know by now that I believe in telling the truth about these things. But if you wanted me to lie, go ahead and wear it. It's lovely and that color doesn't make you look like a pumpkin at all."

Georgie had put it on anyway, just to see if she agreed. She zipped it and looked in the full-length mirror. "Oh, my God, you're right." She got out of it as quickly as she could and threw it into a growing pile of clothes to be given away.

"What was I thinking?"

"Maybe you got it to go to a Halloween party."

"Ha ha. It's a summer dress." She tried on several more, none of which seemed right. Finally, she tried on a deep V-neck blue-and-white slim-fitting floral print dress. The dress flared at the high waist into a flirty, short skirt.

"That's the one," Audrey said.

"You don't think it's too short?" She turned around so she could see the back. "The neckline is kind of low too."

Audrey laughed. "I can guarantee you that Spencer won't think so about either of those things."

Georgie smiled. "You're right about that."

"So I take it all is well in Georgie and Spencer land?"

"All is wonderful."

"Everything still going well at work?"

"Yes. We work really well together and have from the first, but I'll admit I was worried when we first got together. I thought it might change our working relationship."

"Has it?"

"I think it's made us better. We know each other well enough now that we kind of automatically fall into a good rhythm." She looked in the mirror and decided she'd pass. She began to put on makeup. She didn't wear a lot at work but since this was a special occasion—or so Spencer said—it merited more than her usual swipe of mascara and lip gloss.

"I'll get going now," Audrey said. "And I want all the details later."

"Some details," she said with a laugh.

"Spoilsport," Audrey said and left.

A little while later Spencer knocked on her door. He had a key but he always knocked if he thought she'd be there. "Hi, you look great," he said, kissing her hello.

"Thank you." If she hadn't known better she'd have said he was nervous. But Spencer didn't get nervous. "What's up? Where are we going?"

"It's a surprise."

"Don't I get a hint?"

"Nope. Are you ready?"

"Lead on."

She'd had a suspicion when they started out of where they were going but when he turned off the highway she knew she was right. "We're going to the Caldwells'?"

"Yes. I thought about blindfolding you but I figured you'd resist that."

"You figured right." Spencer seemed totally distracted and barely talked as they bumped and jostled along the dirt track that passed for a road. "I see Jethro still hasn't fixed the road."

"He says he likes it this way. His daughter and grand-daughter have tried to talk him into at least fixing the ditch, but he won't hear of it."

He stopped and turned off the truck at the top of the hill just before the famous ditch. "Come on." They both got out and Spencer held out his hand. They walked down to the ditch hand in hand.

"What's going on, Spencer? Why are we here?"

"You'll see. Since it's hotter than Hades out here I didn't bring a picnic or a blanket to sit on. I didn't think we'd be out here that long." He stopped and looked around. "This is it. As close as I can get, anyway."

"Close to what?" she asked, though she suspected she knew.

"Our kiss that night we got stuck." With that he got down on one knee and took hold of her hand.

She could hardly breathe. Her heart was beating a hundred plus miles an hour. She couldn't have spoken if she tried.

"I love you, Georgie. I've loved you since the moment I saw you. I didn't realize it until a little later, but that's the moment I fell in love with you, under the mistletoe when you looked at me and said, 'No way.'"

She laughed. "That's not how I remember it."

"Poetic license." He frowned. "Where was I? Oh, yeah, you said no way and it took about five more times under the mistletoe before you'd kiss me. And when you did I fell in love with you."

"Love at first kiss?" she teased.

"I was already halfway there. The kiss just sealed the deal. But now we've known each other for six months. And I can't imagine my life without you in it. I love you, Georgie. Will you marry me?"

In his other hand he held out a ring. A sparkling round diamond set in platinum, with a baguette on either side. Simple and beautiful. "I love you too. Yes, Spencer, I'll marry you."

He slipped the ring on her finger, then stood and took her in his arms and kissed her. That took some time, but eventually she said, "That was the most romantic thing anyone has ever done for me."

"Damn. I can't believe I forgot. Wait here." He ran back to the truck and returned carrying what looked like a bunch of dried leaves. He held it over both their heads and said, "Kiss me."

"Is that the mistletoe—"

"Yes, from Christmas Eve last year. I saved it."

She threw her arms around his neck and kissed him. "Let's do this every year. At Christmas and six months later."

"Sounds like a deal to me."

The End

If you enjoyed this book, please leave a review at your favorite online retailer! Even if it's just a sentence or two it makes all the difference.

Thanks for reading *Under the Mistletoe* by Eve Gaddy!

Discover your next romance at TulePublishing.com.

TULE
PUBLISHING

If you enjoyed *Under the Mistletoe,*
you'll love the next book in....

The Heart of Texas series

Book 1: *Heart of the Texas Doctor*

Book 2: *Texas on My Mind*

Book 3: *Under the Mistletoe*

Book 4: *Heart of a Texas Warrior*
Coming February 2020!

More books by Eve Gaddy

The Gallaghers of Montana series

Book 1: *Sing Me Back Home*

Book 2: *Love Me, Cowgirl*

Book 3: *The Doctor's Christmas Proposal*

Book 4: *The Cowboy and the Doctor*

Book 5: *Return of the Cowgirl*

The Devil's Rock at Whiskey River series

Book 1: *Rebel Pilot Texas Doctor*

Book 2: *His Best Friend's Sister*

Book 3: *No Ordinary Texas Billionaire*

If you enjoyed *Under the Mistletoe*, you'll love these other Last Stand Christmas books!

Christmas Flowers
by Sasha Summers

Christmas for the Deputy
by Nicole Helm

A Lone Star Christmas
by Justine Davis

About the Author

Eve Gaddy is the best-selling award-winning author of more than seventeen novels. Her books have won and been nominated for awards from Romantic Times, Golden Quill, Bookseller's Best, Holt Medallion, Texas Gold, Daphne Du Maurier and more. She was nominated for a Romantic Times Career Achievement Award for Innovative Series romance as well as winning the 2008 Romantic Times Career Achievement award for Series Storyteller of the year. Eve's books have sold over a million copies worldwide and been published in many foreign countries. Eve lives in East Texas with her husband of many years.

Thank you for reading

Under the Mistletoe

If you enjoyed this book, you can find more from all our great authors at TulePublishing.com, or from your favorite online retailer.

TULE
PUBLISHING

Made in the USA
Columbia, SC
01 November 2021